Praise For
Today I Ate a Biscuit

"The author clearly has a gift for description and setting a mood. His simple word choice and attention to the smallest detail is remarkable as he mines the depths of the textures and taste of his biscuits with droll moments of humor... The story's greatest strength is an understated yet inescapable wistfulness."
— *BlueInk Review*

"As the story progresses in its weird, nearly delusional level of rapt concentration, Davis works hard to invest his readers in the mini-drama of a good biscuit: the anticipation, the consumption, and the baking. He cannily uses dramatic language ('I could see it: that perfect version of myself pulling the tray from the oven') in order to color a story of 'a biscuit worthy of folklore.' As such, the storytelling is unquestionably passionate."
— *Kirkus Reviews*

TODAY I ATE A BISCUIT

Justin M. Davis

Today I Ate a Biscuit

Copyright © 2026 Justin M. Davis

Published by Wayward Scripts
St. Helens, Oregon, USA

All rights reserved. This book or parts thereof may not be reproduced in any form, stored in any retrieval system, or transmitted in any form by any means—electronic, mechanical, photocopy, recording, or otherwise—without prior written permission of the author, except as provided by United States of America copyright law. For permission requests, contact the author at the website below.

ISBN: 978-1-971536-01-9 (e-book)
ISBN: 978-1-971536-00-2 (paperback)
ISBN: 978-1-971536-02-6 (audiobook)

Library of Congress Control Number: 2026901908

This is a work of fiction. All of the biscuits, ingredients, and events portrayed in this novel are either products of the author's imagination or are used fictitiously. No biscuits were consumed during the making of this book.

Visit the author's website at justinmdavis.com

This book is dedicated to my wife and kids who have always supported me in all of my endeavors.

Part One: The Biscuit
- Chapter 1: *The First Bite*
- Chapter 2: *The Second Bite*
- Chapter 3: *The Crumb Situation*
- Chapter 4: *Insignificant Consequences*
- Chapter 5: *The Mid-Biscuit Plateau*
- Chapter 6: *Distractions*
- Chapter 7: *The Last Bite*
- Chapter 8: *Victory, Momentum, and the Mess Ahead*
- Chapter 9: *Post-Biscuit Silence*
- Chapter 10: *Too Late for Butter*

Part Two: Behind the Biscuit
- Chapter 11: *The Hunger That Began It All*
- Chapter 12: *The Fridge, the Pantry, and the Graveyard of Options*
- Chapter 13: *Whisking the Void*
- Chapter 14: *Preheated Expectations*
- Chapter 15: *The Birth of the Biscuit*
- Chapter 16: *Cooling, Judgment, and Acceptance*

Part Three: A Second Biscuit
- Chapter 17: *The Dough Rises Again*
- Chapter 18: *The Cleanup*
- Chapter 19: *A Second Attempt*
- Chapter 20: *A Better Biscuit*
- Chapter 21: *The Second Second Bite*
- Chapter 22: *Nothing Left to Prove*
- Chapter 23: *Final Reflection*

Part One

The Biscuit

CHAPTER 1

The First Bite

Today I ate a biscuit. It was, truthfully, not the most impressive of biscuits. The crust, while flaky, was somewhat bland and unimpressive. Arguably, there was a subtle hint of buttery flavor, though it was so minute as to barely be worth mentioning. Still, a biscuit that promises nothing is at least honest, and there is a kind of comfort in honesty, even when that honesty admits to mediocrity.

I examined it before that first bite, turning it slightly in my hand. The light from the kitchen window fell across its surface, revealing the faint irregularities in its shape—the small cracks where the dough had stretched and split, the uneven browning along the top where the oven's heat had played favorites. At certain angles, it was matte and pale; at others, the faintest glint of golden crust appeared, as though the biscuit were trying, without much confidence, to pass itself off as something better. My thumb traced the higher ridges, their faint warmth giving the shadows shape. There was no artistry in it, but something about its unpolished simplicity held a quiet appeal.

I held it longer than was necessary, letting my thumb trace the edge where the top met the side. The surface was cool now, no trace of the oven's warmth, but I could still feel the faint powdery residue of flour—stubborn, clinging, almost chalk-like. It reminded me this was not a biscuit from a package or a bakery display, smoothed to perfection. This was a biscuit with a history, brief and inelegant as it was, and here I stood at its culmination. Even the air seemed stiller, as though the moment before the first bite required a hush of its own—broken only by the quiet shift of my breath, a reminder that time had not stopped, only slowed.

I turned the biscuit slowly in my hand, as if warmth itself might confess some hidden truth. The surface felt uneven—raised in places like cooling dunes, collapsed in others where the dough had surrendered early. The crust bore small fissures reminiscent of cracked desert clay, the kind that forms when heat and dryness conspire against the earth. One ridge curled upward defiantly; another sagged inward, as though unsure it ever wanted to rise at all.

The color was not uniform, and this, I thought, was a good thing. Perfection is sterile; flaws make a thing real. The edges wore a muted gold, deepening to amber in places where the heat had lingered just a heartbeat too long. The top, however, told a different story—pale in some patches, as though it had shied away from the browning process altogether, content to remain unambitious. At certain tilts, the surface absorbed the light into its matte stillness, the shadows settling into the cracks like ink in old paper. Tilted differently, the flakier ridges gave off a faint shimmer—not a bright catch of light, but something softer, like dust stirred in a sunbeam. It was only the suggestion of preciousness, a half-remembered glimmer the mind provides when reality refuses to.

I studied it the way one might study a photograph of a stranger's face—not for beauty, but for character. It had none of the uniformity of factory-born pastries, none of the glossy, symmetrical perfection that exists to lure you at a glance. No, this was honest in its appearance. It did not pretend to be more than it was, nor less. In its uneven crust, its asymmetrical shape, and its subdued palette, it offered only the truth.

The biscuit sat cool against my palm, the oven's warmth long since surrendered to the air. I no longer felt the powdery residue of flour, yet the memory of it lingered—an emblem of the biscuit's unpolished honesty. When I pressed lightly with my thumb, the crust yielded just enough, neither soft nor hard, like a handshake from someone still deciding their confidence.

A faint creak from the chair beneath me reminded me that time had not paused with me.

It was heavier in the center than at the edges, the weight settling downward as though the biscuit's modest density had gravitated to its core. The outer rim felt lighter, almost fragile, as if the mere pressure of a fingernail might send a flake tumbling away. I let my thumb travel the perimeter slowly, following the uneven rise and fall of its shape, tracing each subtle contour as if committing them to memory.

We often hold things longer than we need to, not out of indecision, but to make the parting slower. Perhaps I lingered for that reason, though I could not say for certain. There is a small ceremony in the moments before an object changes from something you possess to something you consume. The pause is not for the object's sake but for one's own, a way to mark the quiet threshold between wanting and surrender.

They say anticipation heightens the pleasure. I have found this to be true often enough that I take it on faith. A long-awaited letter, a long-nursed bottle of wine, a long-absent friend—the waiting sweetens the moment, making the first taste, the first sip, the first word all the more potent. And so, with my biscuit in hand, I let the moment linger. Not because I am uncertain, nor because I expect greatness, but because this—right here—might be the best this particular biscuit will ever be. Before the reality replaces the idea. Before the truth meets the tongue.

My thoughts wandered, as they tend to do in moments of pause. I remembered other biscuits—dense ones, dry ones, and a few warm enough that their buttery layers glowed in memory if not in fact. I thought about the difference between hunger and desire. Hunger asks only to be answered; desire wants to be courted. Hunger will forgive a poor meal, but desire... desire can be wounded.

For a fleeting instant, I considered not eating it at all —to leave it untouched, preserved as possibility rather than reduced to certainty. A draft stirred the edge of a napkin, reminding me that hesitation, too, must eventually move. After all, it is a rare thing for reality to surpass imagination, and rarer still when one's expectations are already modest.

The room felt quieter in those moments, as though it were waiting too. Light rested still on the table. The air seemed to hesitate. Even my own breath slowed, as though to avoid breaking the fragile balance of this suspended moment.

They say the moment before a thing happens holds more power than the thing itself. I wondered if this was truly that moment—or if I was simply delaying the inevitable out of habit rather than reverence.

I began to lift the biscuit, slowly, as though its movement through the air might disturb the quiet balance that had settled over the room. The angle of the morning light shifted across its surface as it rose, revealing in succession each familiar imperfection I had already studied. The deeper cracks caught shadows, becoming narrow canyons once more, while the flaky ridges caught thin lines of brightness, like the first light touching the peaks of distant hills.

My arm was steady, not with effort but with intent. There was no strain in the muscles, only the deliberate pace of someone determined to grant an object its full procession to the place where it would meet its fate. My other hand remained beneath, palm open, ready to catch whatever fragment might choose this moment to abandon the whole.

One such fragment did, in fact, make its bid for freedom—a small crumb, clinging stubbornly to the edge until gravity's quiet persistence convinced it otherwise. I watched it fall, turning once in the air before it landed on the table with a sound so soft I nearly doubted I had heard it. For an instant, I considered retrieving it, not to eat, but simply to restore it to the biscuit from which it had come, as though reunification could matter to something so insignificant as a crumb off nothing more than a simple biscuit.

The biscuit neared my mouth, and with its nearness the scent grew more distinct. There was the faint, almost shy whisper of butter—not bold enough to announce itself, but there all the same. Underneath it, the warm neutrality of baked flour, and beneath that still, the faintest trace of something slightly overdone, as though a single moment too long in the oven had left its mark. My lips parted in quiet preparation, and my breath shifted—not deeper, not faster, but subtly aware that the distance between biscuit and bite had become very small indeed.

My teeth met the biscuit's crust with a sound that was both sharper and softer than I had expected—a brittle snap that surrendered almost instantly into a muted crumble. The resistance was brief, as though the crust had been holding itself together purely for ceremony, collapsing at the first sign of real contact.

A single fragment broke away before the rest, landing on my tongue like an early arrival to a gathering. It shifted lightly as my jaw moved, its dry weight a reminder that the suspended moment had passed; the bite was now underway.

Several crumbs escaped altogether, slipping free of the biscuit's form and scattering downward. They fell with the quiet urgency of captives making a run for the gate, each one taking its own path toward the table or my lap. I could not help but watch them go, noting how some clung to the edges of my shirt while others vanished into the folds of fabric. In that moment, I thought—not without a faint sense of guilt—that every act of consumption is also an act of destruction, and that the crumbs were the first casualties of this small inevitable conquest.

The first impression was not taste but texture. The biscuit was dry—not unpleasantly so, but insistent, breaking down in uneven rhythms: some fragments dissolving at once, others catching briefly before yielding. A few stubborn bits clung on longer than they had any right to, scratching faintly at the roof of my mouth before they, too, gave in.

Coarse particles of flour pressed against the upper palate of my mouth, their roughness distinct from the softer crumble that surrounded them. They caught in the ridges there, dragging faintly as my tongue moved against them, each pass an exercise in persistence. The warmth of saliva began its slow work, softening the stiffer pieces, drawing them gradually into compliance. What had moments before been brittle and unyielding now yielded, but reluctantly, as though giving in not from choice, but from the steady insistence of time and moisture.

One small crumb, however, had managed to find its way to the back of my tongue, clinging there in quiet defiance. I considered swallowing it as it was, allowing it to go unchallenged into the next stage of its journey. But there was something about the idea that felt unsatisfactory, as though I were conceding a point in an argument I had not yet lost. I pressed my tongue against the roof of my mouth, attempting to coax it forward, but it held its ground with admirable stubbornness. In the end, I let it remain, deciding that some battles, even in matters as small as a biscuit, can be left unresolved without real consequence.

The flavor arrived slowly, as though reluctant to declare itself. The first note was a suggestion of butter—so faint that I wondered, briefly, if it might be nothing more than my own expectation filling in the gap. It was there, but not fully present, like a half-remembered face passing in a crowd.

Beyond that came a middle taste so neutral it defied description. Not unpleasant, certainly, but offering nothing to seize upon, nothing to fix in memory except its own absence of distinction. It was a pause rather than a statement, a stretch of silence between two unremarkable sounds.

Only at the end did a faint saltiness emerge, lingering at the edges of my tongue as though it had arrived late and unsure whether it was meant to be here at all. It did not sharpen the flavor so much as confirm that a flavor had, in fact, existed.

Some things are neither good nor bad, and it is their mediocrity that makes them strangely memorable. This biscuit seemed to understand that truth perfectly, offering nothing in excess and nothing in deficit—existing, simply, in the exact middle of the road.

I became aware, as I chewed the last of that first bite, of just how much thought I had devoted to it. More, I suspected, than most people grant to an entire meal. It seemed almost disproportionate, this level of scrutiny for something so ordinary, so unwilling to meet me halfway in the exchange of pleasure. And yet, here I was, dissecting each moment as though it might uncover some small insight tucked away in the folds of daily life.

The biscuit, for its part, did not pretend to be more than it was. It had offered what it could, modest as that might be, and I found myself accepting it on those terms. There was a kind of peace in that acceptance, a quiet acknowledgment that not all experiences strive toward greatness—some simply exist, and their value lies in having happened at all.

I exhaled slowly, the act feeling less like satisfaction and more like the conclusion of a thought that had gone as far as it could. The moment had passed, leaving nothing behind but a few scattered crumbs and the faint, lingering taste of something that would neither offend nor inspire. It was, in its own way, an ending.

CHAPTER 2
The Second Bite

The biscuit was no longer whole. A small corner was missing now, an absence that altered its symmetry in a way that felt faintly personal, as though I had changed it in a manner that could never be undone. The once unbroken curve of its edge now bore a jagged gap—the quiet, undeniable evidence of the first bite. It was not a dramatic change, but it was enough to shift the entire character of the biscuit. Where before it had seemed complete, now it seemed in progress—a work partially undertaken, its conclusion inevitable but not yet reached.

I found myself looking at it with the faint recognition one has for a place visited twice. The first bite had been an event, marked by ceremony, careful inspection, and anticipation drawn out to its furthest possible length. This second bite lacked that air of discovery. The mystery of the crust's resistance and the crumb's texture was no longer a mystery at all. And yet, familiarity does not erase significance. The first bite was the opening chapter; the second, a continuation—smaller in scope, perhaps, but no less connected to the whole.

No two bites are the same, yet they are part of the same whole. The first had been approached with a kind of reverence, its imperfections observed and cataloged before the teeth had even made contact. Now, I observed the changes those teeth had wrought. The crust around the missing section had fractured in uneven ways, leaving tiny, flaked ridges that caught the light differently than the smoother untouched areas. A few loose crumbs clung stubbornly to the exposed crumb face, as though resisting assimilation into the surrounding air.

I thought of the way I had held it during the first bite, the deliberate slowness with which it had traveled from plate to mouth. This second bite would follow much the same route, yet it already felt different. There was a thread connecting the two moments, but it was not the same thread as before. If the first bite had been a door opening onto unknown ground, the second was the step taken onto a path already seen—still worth walking, but without the surprise of what lay ahead.

The first bite had exposed something new—a part of the biscuit that had, until now, been hidden away, sealed beneath its modest crust. Where before I had studied only the surface, here was the unguarded interior, revealed in cross-section like the inner rings of a felled tree. It was pale, almost off-white, with a faint warmth of color that deepened toward the outer edge where crumb met crust.

The texture was a network of small, uneven air pockets, some wide enough to suggest moments of ambition during baking, others so slight they seemed reluctant to exist at all. I traced their arrangement with my eyes, noting how they clustered and stretched, creating a loose pattern that was both random and deliberate—like sedimentary rock layers shifted by unseen forces. If the crust had been the biscuit's public face, this crumb felt like a private truth: softer, more fragile, and wholly unprepared for the scrutiny it now received.

In some places, the crumb clung to the crust with quiet loyalty, a thin golden edge still holding them together. In others, the separation was more decisive—clean, abrupt, as if the two had never been truly committed to each other in the first place. Tiny flecks of crust had broken free entirely, leaving behind empty impressions like footprints in sand after the tide has withdrawn.

I thought about how much of the first bite had been concerned with the unknown. Now, there was a strange satisfaction in seeing what had been hidden, even if the sight itself was not remarkable. The crumb was not beautiful, nor was it ugly; it simply was—an honest declaration of the biscuit's innermost self. Perhaps this was the truest part of the whole, untouched by the oven's browning or the flour's dusting. And yet, I couldn't help but wonder if knowing the inside so soon might rob the later bites of some small, unspoken mystery.

It was lighter now, though not by much—just enough to be noticed if one paid attention. And I was paying attention. The absence of the first bite had altered more than the biscuit's appearance; it had changed the very way it rested in my hand. Before, its weight had been evenly distributed, a steady, balanced presence against my palm. Now, the center of gravity leaned slightly away from the missing corner, tilting the whole in a way that made it feel less certain of itself.

I adjusted my grip, shifting my fingers upward to support the heavier side. This required a small, almost imperceptible rotation of the wrist, as though I were rebalancing a scale that had been thrown off by a single grain. It was not uncomfortable, but it was different, and difference, however slight, demands accommodation.

The missing section's exposed crumb felt more vulnerable to touch than the smooth, intact crust. My fingertips, brushing against it by accident, left the faintest impression—so faint it was gone almost as soon as I noticed it, yet enough to remind me that what remained was softer, less defended. Holding the biscuit now felt less like grasping an object and more like cradling a thing in mid-transition, no longer whole but not yet gone.

I wondered how many other things in life changed so subtly that we never noticed until we had to adjust our hold on them. The shift here was minor—just a redistribution of weight—but it altered the entire dynamic between biscuit and hand. And as I sat there, making these small accommodations for something so simple, I realized that in this second bite's shadow, the biscuit was no longer quite the same companion it had been a moment before.

They say anticipation heightens the pleasure. I had believed it during the first bite—I'd let the moment stretch, drawn out every possible second before teeth met crust, because it seemed important, even noble, to grant the biscuit that kind of ceremony. Now, with the second bite before me, I found that same phrase drifting back into my mind, but with noticeably less conviction, like an actor returning for a second performance after the opening night has passed.

The first bite had been all possibility. It was a question waiting to be answered, and in answering it, the mystery was lost but the truth revealed. The second bite had no such question to pose; it had already been answered. I knew what the crust would feel like, how the crumb would yield, what faint traces of butter and salt would appear and then quietly retreat. This was not the heady anticipation of the unknown—this was the quieter anticipation of a familiar experience, and I was not sure if that was better or worse.

Some things improve upon repetition. A song you love can grow richer with each hearing, its familiar notes deepening into something almost personal. A well-worn book can reveal new meanings with each reading. But then there are the other things—the jokes that are never as funny the second time, the magic tricks whose secrets you now know, the desserts that taste somehow smaller when you return for a second slice.

I found myself piling metaphors onto the question, as though the right comparison might finally reveal the nature of the second bite.

I lingered there, biscuit in hand, wondering which of these categories the second bite might belong to. Was it a familiar pleasure, mellowed and comfortable? Or was it a diminished echo of what had already been tasted and found wanting? I could not decide. And perhaps that indecision was the only true anticipation left.

I began to lift the biscuit again, though now it presented itself differently. The once smooth arc of its edge had been broken by the first bite, leaving a jagged profile that caught the light in unpredictable ways. The crust's golden ridges no longer formed a continuous line; instead, they rose and fell unevenly, like the peaks and valleys of a low mountain range viewed from a great distance—if such a range were made of flour, butter, and restraint.

As the biscuit rose, I noticed how the light pooled in the exposed crumb, soaking into its porous texture rather than glinting off it as it had with the crust. There was a kind of quiet humility in that—the crumb did not try to shine, only to exist. A small piece of it, clinging near the jagged edge, trembled with each incremental movement upward. For a moment I thought it might hold, but gravity, patient and inevitable, claimed it. The crumb drifted down in a slow, meandering fall, finally settling on the plate below.

I considered whether the uneven edge made this bite more or less dignified. There was an honesty in it—a refusal to pretend perfection after the first bite had left its mark. And yet, there was also something faintly disheveled about it, as if the biscuit were showing up to an important occasion with its collar askew. Perhaps dignity was not in the appearance but in the manner of approach, and so I held it with the same care as before, determined that the lack of symmetry would not diminish the ceremony of the moment.

My teeth met the biscuit's soft interior before they reached the crust—a reversal from the first bite, and one that immediately changed the experience. The crumb yielded at once, collapsing without even the token resistance the crust had offered before. It was like stepping onto sand after walking across stone—a transition so abrupt it felt momentarily disorienting.

The crust came later, a secondary note rather than the opening chord, and when it did arrive it offered only a brief, brittle snap before giving way. There was no drama in its surrender, only a quiet acknowledgment that its role in this bite was supporting rather than leading.

Midway through, a small fragment of crumb detached from the main body and began drifting toward my cheek. Without thinking, my tongue moved to intercept it—a swift, practiced motion born from a lifetime of preventing errant morsels from escaping. I trapped it before it could slip further, pressing it gently against the roof of my mouth until it rejoined the rest of the bite. The whole event lasted perhaps a second, yet it carried with it the faint satisfaction of a narrowly averted loss, as though I had rescued something worth keeping.

The interior crumb absorbed moisture with far greater speed than the crust ever had. Almost instantly, it began to soften, its structure collapsing into something smoother, less distinct. This was a change without a clear verdict—on one hand, the quick surrender meant less dryness, a certain immediate comfort. On the other, it shortened the experience, robbing the bite of the slow, drawn-out transformation the crust had demanded. I found myself unable to decide whether this was an improvement or simply a shortcut, the kind that leaves you wondering if something essential was lost along the way.

As I considered this, my attention was drawn—with an urgency far greater than the situation deserved—to a new development. A small fragment of crumb had lodged itself between two of my teeth. It was not painful, nor even particularly uncomfortable, yet its presence was undeniable. I shifted my tongue to investigate, and in doing so, I was reminded of an older problem: the obstinate crumb from the first bite, still clinging to the back of my tongue as if it had taken up a long-term lease.

Now there were two of them—one an established tenant, the other a newly arrived intruder—and for a moment I pictured them as conspirators, whispering to one another in the dark recesses of my mouth. I debated taking action, perhaps dislodging them both in a single, decisive sweep. But the thought of interrupting the bite's progression felt wrong, as though it would break some unspoken contract between the biscuit and I. So I let them be, content—or at least resigned—to their quiet occupation.

The flavor arrived just as I remembered it—the faintest suggestion of butter, almost shy in its presentation, followed by the neutral, unremarkable middle, and finally the quiet afterthought of salt. There was no need to search for it this time; I knew where each note would appear, as if the biscuit were following a script it had already performed once before.

It was like rereading a sentence you only half-remember. The words are the same, and perhaps even more clearly understood the second time, but the surprise is gone. The small hesitations, the wonder of not knowing what might come next—all of it replaced by the certainty of recognition.

Predictability can be comfort, or it can be boredom. The difference often lies not in the thing itself but in the one experiencing it. And as I chewed the second bite, I found myself suspended between the two. There was a reassurance in knowing exactly what I would get, but also a faint disappointment in realizing that it could offer nothing more. It was the same biscuit, the same flavor, the same restrained performance—and perhaps that was the point.

The second bite had done nothing to change my opinion of the biscuit. It had not improved upon the first, nor had it diminished it. It simply was—another small step along a path whose destination I could already see. There was no great revelation in it, no sudden shift in perception. The biscuit had revealed itself in the first bite, and the second had merely confirmed the truth of what I already knew.

Still, I found myself pausing, biscuit in hand, considering whether to continue. It was not that I doubted my ability to finish it—the thing was hardly a feat of endurance—but rather that I questioned the necessity of doing so. The biscuit was unremarkable, and its remaining portions would likely be no different from what I had already experienced. And yet, there was a certain logic to pressing on.

I weighed my options briefly, imagining the biscuit abandoned halfway, sitting on the plate as a monument to my disinterest. That seemed almost worse than finishing it. Perhaps there was value in seeing something through, even if only for the satisfaction of completion. After all, a journey once begun feels incomplete if left unfinished, no matter how uninspiring the scenery along the way.

If the first bite was an introduction, the second was simply a confirmation. And having made it this far, I might as well finish.

CHAPTER 3
The Crumb Situation

The biscuit was still there, though in truth it was no longer the biscuit it had been. Two bites had reduced it not only in size but in integrity. Its edges were less certain, its shape compromised, its symmetry irrevocably altered. And yet, the change to the biscuit itself was only part of the story.

The rest of the story lay scattered about me. On the plate, small flecks of crust and crumb clung to the surface as if reluctant to be swept away. On my lap, a modest but noticeable sprinkling of fragments had gathered, forming an irregular constellation against the fabric of my trousers. My shirt, once pristine, now bore its own dusting—a light scattering of particles so fine they seemed almost woven into the cloth itself. And beyond these, there was the floor, where an errant handful of microscopic debris had already begun forming their own loose and disorganized colonies.

The biscuit, then, was no longer confined to the space it occupied. It had expanded, in its own way, to claim territory far beyond the plate. It was no longer a single, coherent object but a collection of scattered pieces—some recoverable, others already lost to the world. The scene before me was less a meal in progress and more the aftermath of an event, one that demanded not mere observation but careful, deliberate documentation.

My shirt had not begun the day with any particular significance. It was merely the shirt I happened to be wearing—clean, unassuming, and entirely unconnected to the matter of the biscuit. And yet now, it had become part of the story.

Across the fabric lay a fine scattering of golden flecks, each one small enough to seem harmless, yet numerous enough to be unmistakable. Some rested loosely on the surface, ready to be brushed away with the lightest touch. Others, however, had found purchase, clinging as though the weave of the cloth itself had welcomed them in. I tried a casual swipe with my palm and found that these more determined intruders did not so much as shift, remaining fixed in place with a quiet stubbornness that felt disproportionate to their size.

It was difficult to say whether these crumbs were truly on the shirt, or whether, in settling there, they had already begun to become the shirt. The difference seemed academic at best, yet the thought lingered—that perhaps this garment, once simply an article of clothing, was now an artifact, altered in some small but permanent way by the biscuit's passing.

If the crumbs on my shirt were a light dusting, then the ones on my lap were a full encampment. Larger in size and fewer in number, they had gathered across my thighs as if convening for some unspoken purpose. Their positions were irregular but deliberate, scattered in such a way that I could not help but imagine them plotting— each crumb holding its ground while keeping a respectful distance from the others, like generals in council.

Some rested confidently in the open, their weight and position making them unlikely to move without deliberate interference. Others were less secure, balanced precariously on the folds of fabric where the slightest shift in posture could send them tumbling to the floor. I became acutely aware of my own stillness, as though any movement might disrupt the fragile stability of their current arrangement.

I considered my options. I could attempt to brush them into my hand and return them to the plate, though such an operation risked dislodging the less secure crumbs and losing them entirely. I could make a quick, decisive movement to shake them free all at once, allowing gravity to do its work and the floor to claim them. Or I could simply wait, letting time and chance dictate which crumbs would remain and which would fall. In the end, I chose inaction, holding my position as if observing the outcome of their silent conference might, in some way, be important.

Below me, the floor had begun to collect its share of the biscuit's remains. Not in neat clusters or uniform lines, but in an irregular scattering that brought to mind the haphazard spread of an untrained militia—an army of tiny crumbs, each occupying its own patch of territory, united only by their shared displacement.

They were smaller than their counterparts on my lap and shirt, so small in fact that I began to wonder if they might be beneath the notice of even a mouse. A mouse, having braved the journey into this room with expectations of some modest feast, would find instead a meager offering—specks of crust barely worth the trouble of gathering. I could almost picture its tiny face, ears twitching in muted disappointment, before it turned away in search of better prospects.

Meanwhile, the crumbs on my shirt and trousers seemed to hover in a state of indecision. Some clung more tightly to the weave of the fabric, perhaps sensing that to fall would be to join the beleaguered ranks below, subject to the same uncertain fate as those already on the floor. Others appeared poised to let go at any moment, as if drawn by some unspoken call to swell the numbers of the growing army below. Whether this reluctance to join was born out of some misplaced loyalty to the biscuit or simply the will to remain intact a moment longer, I could not say.

The table was home to its own set of survivors. Here the crumbs were neither as numerous as those on the floor nor as tenacious as those clinging to my clothing, but they occupied a strategic position—close enough to be easily retrieved, yet spread far enough apart to make any effort at collection feel deliberate.

Some were large enough to tempt retrieval, intact enough to offer at least the suggestion of a final, miniature bite. Others were so minuscule that the thought of lifting them felt almost futile, as though their removal would yield nothing more than the satisfaction of tidiness. Together they formed an irregular front line, scattered across the grain of the wood like scouts who had ventured too far from the main force.

I considered the moral implications of eating crumbs directly from the table. On one hand, they were, undeniably, part of the biscuit, and leaving them behind seemed almost wasteful. On the other, they now bore the subtle imprint of the table's surface—a mingling of worlds that made their reclamation feel somehow improper.

If this was to become a battle, the table's contingent would be the most immediate threat, positioned within striking distance should I choose to act. Between them, the encamped crumbs on my lap, and the growing militia amassing on the floor, I was surrounded on multiple fronts. The eventual cleanup would not be a simple sweeping gesture but a campaign—one fought in stages, with the knowledge that victory could never be absolute.

Nothing lasts forever—not even the smallest piece of a whole. And yet, in these scattered remnants, the biscuit continued to assert its presence, stubbornly refusing to vanish without effort.

Far from the main field of crumbs, I spotted it—a lone fragment, exiled from the others by some unpredictable combination of momentum and gravity. It had rolled further than any of its companions, coming to rest just beyond the shadow cast by the table's edge, as though deliberately distancing itself from the scene of the larger disaster.

Its isolation made it conspicuous. There was no camouflage here, no surrounding debris to blend into, only the pale openness of the floor and one small, stubborn piece of biscuit that seemed content to remain where it had landed. I leaned slightly to get a better look, and it was then that I realized how unremarkable it truly was—neither the largest nor the smallest crumb, lacking any distinctive shape or color, nothing to suggest that it warranted special attention. And yet there it sat, still undeniably part of the biscuit, a quiet reminder that even the most insignificant pieces have a way of demanding notice.

I debated leaving it where it was. Retrieving it would require movement, effort, a deliberate interruption to the stillness I had been maintaining. And really, what would be gained? It was, after all, a crumb—one of many—and not even a particularly notable one. But the longer I looked at it, the more it seemed to hold its ground with a kind of quiet defiance, as though the biscuit itself had planted it there to taunt me.

In the end, I reached for it. My fingers closed around it with the same care one might use to pick up something fragile, though it offered no resistance. I held it for a moment, studying it as if to confirm that this was, in fact, worth the trouble I had taken. It was not. And yet, there was a faint satisfaction in reclaiming it—not because it had value, but because the biscuit would not have the last word.

I began the process of brushing the crumbs from my shirt and lap, expecting it to be a quick, efficient operation. It was not. Some crumbs, perhaps sensing their imminent removal, gave way easily, tumbling down to join the floor's already disorganized ranks. Others resisted, lodging more firmly into the weave of the fabric, crumbling further under my touch so that each attempt to remove them became a self-defeating gesture, scattering the biscuit's remains into smaller, less manageable pieces.

In this way, the biscuit maintained its presence, refusing to be reduced to nothing. Even as I tried to reclaim my once-pristine clothing, it found new ways to cling to me, leaving behind traces that would likely remain until laundry day.

I reflected, in that moment, on the impermanence of form. A crumb, small and fragile, can break down further still, until it is little more than dust—and yet even dust persists. Perhaps nothing ever truly disappears; it only changes shape, becoming something else, somewhere else. The biscuit had been whole, and now it was many—too many, in fact, to be dealt with in a single effort.

In the end, I did what I could. A few of the larger crumbs were close enough, intact enough, to warrant retrieval. I placed them back on the plate and ate them as though they were legitimate bites, giving them a respect they had done nothing to earn. They tasted exactly as expected—dry, faintly salty, and otherwise indistinguishable from the rest of the biscuit. But in eating them, I felt as though I had reclaimed something, however small, from the slow disassembly of the whole.

The others, I allowed to be discarded. Some were too small to bother with, no more than dust; others had fallen into places where retrieval would require more effort than I was prepared to give. These I ignored entirely, consigning them to the inevitable sweep of a cloth or broom at some later time.

And then there were the ones I knew would remain. They would linger unnoticed until the table was wiped or the floor swept—until some future moment when their presence would be revealed not as a memory of this biscuit, but as an inconvenience. In that way, even in absence, the biscuit would continue to exert its quiet influence, long after the last bite had been taken.

The biscuit sat on the plate, diminished but not gone. Its remaining portion was still recognizable as the same unremarkable creation I had begun with, yet its reach had extended well beyond itself. Its fragments were scattered across the table, embedded in my clothing, lying in quiet disarray on the floor. The biscuit's presence could no longer be measured by the space it occupied, but by the territory it had claimed.

In the end, the biscuit's story was not only in what remained, but in what had scattered. It had taken something simple and extended it into a small, sustained campaign—one fought in crumbs and flecks, each demanding more attention than the whole had ever deserved.

I looked at what was left of it and made my decision. I would finish the biscuit. Not out of curiosity—I already knew everything there was to know about it. Not out of hunger—there were other, better things I could eat. And certainly not out of pleasure—the biscuit had offered little of that from the start.

No, I would finish it out of principle. Out of a quiet, stubborn desire to have the last word. This biscuit had taken more of my time and energy than it had earned, and I would not leave it sitting there, smug in its half-eaten state, believing it had inconvenienced me into surrender.

If there was to be a victor in this small, absurd battle, I will not let it go to the biscuit.

CHAPTER 4
Insignificant Consequences

The biscuit was smaller now—smaller, but not weaker. Its form had been diminished by two deliberate bites, its once-whole shape fractured and exposed, yet its presence somehow felt larger than before. It had expanded its reach in ways that no reasonable observer would have predicted, claiming territory well beyond the boundaries of the plate.

The evidence was everywhere. My shirt carried its dusting of gold, my lap an organized camp of larger fragments. The table, once neutral ground, had become a contested zone, dotted with crumbs that dared me to remove them. And the floor—the floor had surrendered entirely, littered with tiny remnants like a field after some small, inconsequential battle.

I could not say for certain whether the biscuit had intended this. It did not strike me as a creature of foresight or malice in the way a truly vindictive pastry might be. And yet, here was the undeniable truth: it had made a mess of things. Whether by accident or quiet design, it had scattered itself across my environment in a display of passive-aggressive persistence. A less remarkable biscuit might have been eaten, enjoyed or not, and then forgotten. But this one seemed determined to leave an impression—not in taste, but in the inconvenient labor it had sown.

If one were to draw a map of the biscuit's influence, it would not be confined to the neat, circular borders it once held. Its dominion now stretched outward in irregular territories, each with its own distinct population and character.

To the north lay the Dusting on the Shirt—a lightly settled region where the biscuit's presence was subtle but undeniable. Golden flecks clung to the fabric in scattered formation, most too small to be gathered by hand yet too numerous to ignore. They seemed content to remain there, secure in the knowledge that their removal would require a dedicated effort, the kind reserved for laundry day.

Directly below, in the midlands, sprawled The Encampment on the Lap—a collection of larger, more organized fragments, their positions suggesting a deliberate arrangement. These were the biscuit's sturdy remnants, holding their ground until such time as I chose to shake them free or gather them up. A few rested in precarious balance on the folds of cloth, prepared to defect to the floor at the slightest disturbance.

Eastward, on the Table, a sparse front line held its ground. These were the visible outposts, scattered along the wood grain like watchmen stationed at uneven intervals. They were within easy reach—almost provocatively so—as if daring me to breach the table's unspoken etiquette and consume them where they lay.

And finally, far to the south, stretched the Crumb Militia of the Floor—a disorganized but numerous force, spread thin across the open expanse. They had no cohesion, no shared defense, yet in sheer number they represented the largest portion of the biscuit's scattered influence. Too small to be reclaimed individually, they would remain in place until swept into oblivion, silent sentinels to the biscuit's passing.

Taken together, these territories formed a patchwork realm, a fragmented empire carved out by a biscuit that had never sought glory but had, through some quiet stubbornness, claimed it all the same.

It is strange how something so small, so unremarkable, can extend its reach far beyond what its form would suggest. One does not expect a biscuit—particularly a biscuit as steadfastly mediocre as this—to alter the shape of its surroundings. And yet, here it was: leaving its mark not in the moment of consumption, but in the subtle, persistent ripples that followed.

It reminded me of the way certain moments in life take on a greater weight than we ever intended. A casual remark, spoken without thought, can echo for years in someone else's memory. A small oversight in judgment can grow into a chain of events no one could have predicted. Entire relationships, careers, even lifetimes have been shifted by things that, at the time, seemed as trivial as... well, an unassuming crumb off an otherwise unremarkable biscuit.

And here I sat, surrounded by evidence that the same truth applied to the domestic sphere. My once clean shirt now bore a dusting that spoke of mild neglect. My lap, until recently unmarked, now hosted an organized encampment of crumbs. The table and floor had been transformed into territories occupied by a force that neither sought nor required my consent.

If it were another biscuit—a grander biscuit, worthy of celebration—perhaps such consequences would feel earned, the mess a worthy testament to its greatness. But this was no such biscuit. This was a biscuit content in its unremarkableness, steady and unassuming in its presentation, yet quietly ambitious in the scope of its aftermath. It had made no noise, declared no intentions, yet it had expanded itself into a series of small inconveniences that together formed something larger, something... lasting.

And that, I thought, was the way of many things in life: greatness may be remembered, but it is often the quiet, persistent disruptions that linger longest.

Some crumbs will vanish quickly. A brush of the hand, a sweep of a cloth, and they are gone—erased without ceremony, without resistance. These are the easy ones, the willing departures, the pieces of the biscuit that accept their fate and move quietly into whatever comes next.

But others will linger. They wedge themselves into the weave of clothing, hiding in plain sight until dislodged by chance hours or even days later. They find their way into the narrow seams of the table, or nestle themselves between the floorboards where no casual effort will reach them. They will not be seen until the next thorough cleaning, when their discovery will be met not with recognition, but with the faint annoyance reserved for things that have overstayed their welcome.

In this way, the biscuit maintains its presence long after its body has been consumed. It is not the size of the crumb that determines its endurance, but its location and its stubbornness. Some things leave not because they are big, but because they are patient. The biscuit seems to understand this intuitively, though I cannot imagine it gave the matter much thought—perhaps persistence is simply part of its nature.

It is strange to think that, days from now, I may be reminded of this moment not by memory of its taste, but by the sight of a single crumb lodged in the hem of a shirt, or by the quiet discovery of a fragment beneath the leg of the table. The biscuit will have passed, yet its influence will remain—a small, steadfast presence that refuses to be entirely forgotten.

By now, the biscuit's flavor had already begun to fade from memory. Not because it was unpleasant—unpleasant things tend to linger far longer—but because it was so thoroughly unremarkable. The taste had offered nothing worth remembering, nothing worth replaying in the mind. And yet, despite this absence of gustatory distinction, the biscuit persisted in my awareness.

It was not the eating of it that kept it alive in my thoughts, but the consequences. The golden flecks on my shirt, the regiment on my lap, the scattered sentinels across the table, the stubborn militia entrenched on the floor—these were the true monuments to the biscuit's passing. The taste was gone, but the mess remained—stubborn and steadfast in its resolve to further inconvenience me.

It occurred to me that life often works this way. We think it is the great moments we will remember—the achievements, the celebrations, the rare joys. But more often, it is the small, unexpected consequences of things that stay with us. The brief comment that turns into a story retold for years. The seemingly trivial decision that alters the shape of a day, or a week, or an entire life. The biscuit was no grand event, but it had left its mark all the same.

And perhaps that was why I felt a faint, simmering resolve beginning to form. Not the resolve of hunger—I was no longer eating this biscuit to satisfy appetite. Not the resolve of desire—I had no great wish for its flavor. No, what I felt now was something quieter, more deliberate. I would finish this biscuit not because it deserved to be finished, but because it had inconvenienced me, and I could not allow such a simple and unremarkable biscuit a victory no matter how small or inconsequential. I will finish this biscuit and claim that victory for myself.

The decision was made. I would finish this biscuit. Not for the pleasure of it—there was none to be had. Not for nourishment—there were other, better foods within reach. No, this would be a victory of principle. A quiet, deliberate reclaiming of the balance of power.

Yet I could not deny that the crumbs had already claimed their own small triumphs. They had spread themselves across my shirt and trousers, infiltrated the folds of fabric, and scattered themselves upon the table and floor. They had secured footholds in my environment that would outlast the biscuit itself, persisting until cleaning day or chance discovery. These victories could not be undone.

Still, there was one prize the biscuit could not keep: itself. Whatever pieces remained whole, I would take from it, bite by bite, until nothing remained but its scattered remnants. It might win its petty battles, but the war—such as it was—would end in my favor. And so, with the quiet resolve of one who has been inconvenienced more than the occasion warrants, I set my mind to the task ahead.

CHAPTER 5
The Mid-Biscuit Plateau

The novelty had gone. The biscuit, once a curiosity worthy of prolonged inspection and theatrical delay, was now just... there. It no longer represented possibility, only inevitability. Where the first bites had carried ceremony, this middle stretch offered only the quiet certainty that it would have to be finished eventually—not because it promised anything, but because it existed.

It reminded me of hobbies I had once begun with great enthusiasm—the half-painted model ship gathering dust, the knitted scarf abandoned halfway along its length, the novel on the nightstand whose bookmark had not moved in months. Those things had started brightly, full of intention and promise, only to stall in the flat middle where the charm wore thin and the work remained.

The difference, of course, was that the biscuit was a simpler project. There would be no months-long return to this, no brushing off of accumulated dust. It could be finished in minutes if I chose, and perhaps that was reason enough to press on. There was still the matter of the mess it had made, after all, and it seemed almost wasteful to suffer the inconvenience of crumbs without seeing the task through. To stop now would be to discard the remainder and leave the work unfinished—a small but undeniable defeat.

And this was not just any biscuit, however unremarkable it might seem. This was a biscuit of my own making, the result of my own effort and time. That alone lent it a weight beyond its taste, however bland that taste may be. I looked at what was left and felt the faintest flicker of camaraderie.

"We started this journey together," I said softly to the biscuit, "so let's finish it together—as allies, not enemies."

I took the next bite not with anticipation, nor with any real desire, but because it needed to be done. There comes a point in any undertaking where the momentum is no longer driven by excitement, only by the quiet understanding that completion is the only way forward. This bite was such a point—a functional gesture in service of the larger goal of being finished.

The taste, unsurprisingly, was unchanged. If anything, its predictability dulled it further. The faint trace of butter, the bland middle, the ghost of salt at the end—all exactly where they had been before, as though the biscuit had memorized its lines and delivered them without variation. Yet, there was something in that consistency that struck me differently now. It was not good, but neither was it bad. It simply was. And perhaps, in a way, that was its own small success.

After all, this was my biscuit. Not purchased, not gifted, but made by my own hands. Whatever its flaws—and they were many—it was still a thing I had brought into being. In that sense, its mediocrity felt less like a disappointment and more like a quiet, modest proof that I could create something at all. A lesser biscuit made by my effort was, in some strange way, better than a perfect biscuit made by someone else.

I chewed slowly, not to savor the flavor, but to mark the moment. This was not just another bite moving the story along—it was a reminder that even the most unremarkable things can carry a weight beyond their qualities when they are ours.

There is a peculiar sameness to the middle of any journey. The start holds the novelty—the sense of stepping into something new. The end carries the promise of closure—the satisfaction of arriving. But the middle? The middle is where time slows, where each step feels much like the one before, and where the only thing ahead is more of what you've already done.

I thought of long drives across flat country, where the horizon never seems to get any closer and the scenery repeats itself like a lazy background in an old cartoon. I thought of the middle years of a job, where you know your tasks well enough to perform them without thought, yet not so well that they bring you any joy. I thought of conversations that begin in a flurry of interest, only to settle into an awkward quiet where neither party has the heart to end it nor the spark to continue.

Even life itself seems to have its middle stretch—a span between the eager beginnings and the reflective endings, where days blur together in the simple act of moving forward without ceremony.

And so it was with the biscuit. The thrill of the first bite had passed, the determination of the second and third reduced to mechanical progress. The plateau had arrived. Each bite from here to the end would be much the same as the last. No new flavors would emerge, no hidden qualities reveal themselves. There was only the task, the plate, and the slow diminishment of the thing before me.

I briefly smiled at the absurdity of it—that this was not the midpoint of a great journey, a novel, or a grand expedition, but of a biscuit. An unremarkable biscuit, whose greatest adventure thus far had been spreading itself in crumbs across my immediate environment. And yet, here I was, feeling the same quiet weight of the middle stretch as if it were any of those greater things.

They say you should save the best bite for last, to end on a high note. But this presented a problem: none of the bites so far had been particularly good. There was no standout morsel to anticipate, no corner or crumb promising to be exceptional. The biscuit was, from edge to center, a uniform plainness.

Still, I wondered if perhaps the idea of the "best bite" could be redefined. Maybe these middle bites were, in their own quiet way, the best after all. Not because they offered any new flavor or texture—they were every bit as bland and unremarkable as those that came before—but because they came after the decision had been made to see this biscuit through.

By this point, I had resolved myself to accept the biscuit for what it was: a micro-accomplishment born of my desire to make a biscuit at all. It was not perfect, and it was certainly not great, but neither was it bad. And in the small world of first attempts, "not bad" is its own modest triumph. These bites were the living proof of that—edible evidence that I could create something functional, if not yet exceptional.

Perhaps it was better this way. If the biscuit had turned out perfect on my first try, then no matter how rich its flavor or how flawless its texture, the achievement would have been diminished by ease. Perfection too soon can make the task itself seem trivial, the victory unearned. A mediocre biscuit, on the other hand, holds promise. It leaves space for improvement, for refinement, for another attempt that builds upon the lessons hidden in its unremarkable form.

And so, while I could not save the "best" bite for last in the usual sense, I could savor the knowledge that even mediocrity, when approached with purpose, had its own strange satisfaction.

For a few bites, I even felt something like peace—a quiet acceptance of the biscuit's mediocrity and a recognition of its modest worth. For a moment, I let myself rest in that thought, as if I had stumbled onto some small truth worth keeping.

Then, mid-bite, reality intruded. My jaw slowed, and I stopped halfway through the motion, the biscuit still resting in my hand. Whatever sense of purpose I had felt in the last mouthfuls was quickly tempered by the simple fact that I was, in the end, still eating a rather bland biscuit.

I considered, for a fleeting moment, setting it down for good. The benefits were obvious: the crumbs' territorial advance would halt, sparing my shirt, lap, table, and floor from further encroachment. The unchanging flavor would no longer demand my polite attention. I could declare the experience "close enough" to finished and move on with my day.

But there was one problem. Stopping now would leave the biscuit standing—not literally, of course, but in spirit. It would remain, untouched and intact in part, a quiet monument to its own unremarkable endurance. The thought of leaving such an enemy—and yes, it had become an enemy in its own passive way—with even a partial victory was intolerable.

No. If the biscuit were to be defeated, it would be defeated entirely. Whatever satisfaction it had stolen from me in taste, I would reclaim in finality. I resumed chewing, each bite now less about the flavor and more about the slow, deliberate claiming of ground.

I adjusted my grip on the biscuit, not because it had grown heavier—if anything, it was noticeably lighter now—but because I wanted to feel it firmly in my hand. There was no more room for dithering, no further pause for reflection. The time for idle philosophy was ending; the time for action had come.

It was not inspiration that drove me now, nor hunger, nor pleasure. This was resolve stripped down to its bare frame—the simple determination to finish what I had started, to see this biscuit through to its inevitable end. I would take each bite, bland as it might be, with the same measured pace, not lingering long enough to let the crumbs spread further, not pausing long enough for the novelty to wear down even more.

I thought of the mess waiting for me—the scattered territories across shirt, lap, table, and floor. I could not clean until the battle was over, and the battle would not be over until the biscuit was gone. Completion meant not just the end of eating, but the beginning of restoration, the return to a clean plate and a crumb-free domain. That alone was reason enough to press forward.

In my mind, the finish line was already in sight. A few more bites, and I would have claimed my small, meaningless victory over this persistently unremarkable adversary.

Yes, I told myself, I would be done soon.

I looked at the biscuit and felt a small, almost reluctant wave of relief. Its size was now manageable, its defeat inevitable. The hardest part was behind me—the novelty, the plateau, the pauses—all that remained was the straightforward task of finishing it. A few more bites and it would be over.

I imagined the final morsel, the last crumb cleared from the plate. The simple satisfaction of setting the plate aside and brushing away the remnants. The moment when I could stand, survey my reclaimed territory, and know that the biscuit was no more.

"I'll be done soon enough," I thought, the words quiet and certain, as though speaking them made them true.

But the world has a cruel sense of irony and a devious way of testing such certainty.

CHAPTER 6
Distractions

I had only just settled into the comforting certainty that I would be done soon enough when the world, in its cruel sense of irony and devious way of testing such certainty, decided otherwise. From the living room came the sharp, insistent trill of my phone—not the gentle chime of a notification, but the full, unrelenting ring of an incoming call.

The sound cut through my focus like a dropped plate in a quiet restaurant. It was jarring, intrusive, and perfectly timed to dismantle the fragile rhythm I had built in the solemn work of biscuit consumption. For a moment, I sat completely still, as if refusing to acknowledge it might make the ringing stop. It did not.

Had the phone been within reach, I might have answered without much thought. But no—it was in the living room, on the far end of the couch where I had abandoned it earlier. To answer would require leaving the table, the plate, and—most troubling—the biscuit.

I hesitated. There is always that moment in any ringing phone's life when you weigh the possible significance of the call against the effort of answering it. Could it be important news? Could it be urgent? Could it be nothing more than another automated voice offering to extend my car's nonexistent warranty?

And yet, there it was, calling for me. The biscuit sat silently before me, perhaps even smugly, as if aware of how quickly my attention could be diverted. I had only seconds to decide: let it ring and risk missing something vital, or get up and meet whatever awaited me in the living room—even at the cost of breaking the biscuit's gaze.

The phone kept ringing, each chime another tap on the thin pane of my resolve. I considered ignoring it. The odds were strong—overwhelmingly so—that the call was nothing of consequence. And yet, there was that small, stubborn voice that always insists, What if?

What if it was important?

What if it was urgent?

What if someone, somewhere, genuinely needed me in this moment—and my failure to answer would become a regret replayed for years?

I tried to reason with myself. The biscuit, after all, was right here. The phone was in the living room. Logic suggested that my priority should remain with the task at hand: finish the biscuit, reclaim the table from the crumbs, and restore order to my surroundings. And yet, the phone's call seemed to carry the weight of possible consequence, the way a knock on the door makes you imagine either a friend or a debt collector waiting on the other side.

I glanced at the biscuit. It sat there, unblinking, unmoving, but not unknowing. If ever a baked good could exude an air of quiet satisfaction, this was it. It knew that if I got up now, I would be leaving it unattended, exposed, vulnerable. Perhaps it even relished the thought that my absence could be its moment to stage another territorial expansion—more crumbs drifting into previously unclaimed territory.

Still, the phone rang. My options dwindled. With a reluctant sigh, I placed the biscuit back on the plate. I adjusted it slightly, as if positioning it for defense in my absence, though from what and from whom I could not say. One last glance, and I rose from my seat, leaving it behind to answer the summons from the living room.

I reached the phone just as the ring broke off into that dead, anticipatory silence before a connection is made. I swiped to answer, bringing it to my ear with the faintest hope that this disruption might at least justify itself.

There was nothing. No telemarketer mispronouncing my name. No surveyor asking for "just a few moments of your time." Not even the hollow voice of a debt collector insisting they'd tried to reach me about some obscure obligation. Just... silence.

I waited, because silence has a way of feeling like a prelude to something. I imagined the faint rustle of breath, the click of a muted microphone, the clearing of a throat—but no sound came. Whoever had called was gone, if they had been there at all.

A wave of irritation rose in me, sharp and untempered. I had left my chair, abandoned the biscuit, and crossed the threshold into the living room for this—for absolutely nothing. And in that nothing, I could almost sense the faintest echo of amusement, as though the biscuit itself were sitting back in the kitchen, watching the clock, knowing it had stolen these precious moments from me.

The phone, still pressed to my ear, gave no response. I ended the call, the screen returning to black, and stood there for a beat longer than necessary—not because I expected anything to happen, but because I needed that pause to properly absorb the absurdity of what had just occurred.

I had gained nothing. The biscuit meanwhile had gained time, and in that time it reclaimed some of its lost power over me.

The phone, now silent and smug in its own way, sat on the far cushion of the couch—exactly where I had left it earlier in my casual neglect. Retrieving it had been simple enough: a lean forward, a stretch of the arm, a brief shift in weight. Yet somehow, in that movement, the biscuit had found a new opportunity for expansion.

There, just beside the couch leg, lay a single crumb. Not an accidental speck carelessly dropped, but a deliberate envoy.

The physics of its arrival here were... suspect. Had it clung stubbornly to my clothing during my earlier bites, biding its time until I ventured into this unclaimed territory? Had some unseen draft carried it across the threshold between kitchen and living room? Or—and I could not entirely dismiss this—had it rolled of its own accord, inch by inch, like some small but determined explorer setting out to discover new lands?

Its choice of landing zone was strategic. The living room was no mere outpost—it was a sanctuary. And the couch... the couch was a fortress. Crumbs that enter its folds do not return. They burrow deep into the seams, weaving themselves into the very fabric, lying in wait for years. Even the most rigorous vacuuming leaves some behind, relics of meals long forgotten. It was entirely possible that this crumb, insignificant as it appeared now, would outlast the couch itself—a stowaway destined to accompany the furniture into another home, another life, another unsuspecting lap.

I could almost imagine it lying there when the couch was one day dismantled or discarded, an ancient remnant of the Great Biscuit Conflict, still intact enough to be recognized for what it was.

This was no mere accident. This was an infiltration. This, beyond all reasoning and rational thought, felt deliberate and intentional. As if the biscuit, in all of its unassuming plainness, was now taunting me.

Back in the kitchen, I stood over the plate, looking down at the biscuit as one might look at an adversary who refuses to yield. It was smaller now, visibly diminished, but in its reduction it seemed to have condensed its will. The invasion of the living room had proven that.

The thought occurred to me—unbidden, but persistent—that I could end this now. The trash can stood only a few feet away, its lid slightly ajar, as if inviting the biscuit to its final rest. A swift motion, a soft thud, and the conflict would be over. No more bland bites. No more crumbs colonizing distant lands.

There was a certain appeal in the idea. Mercy, perhaps. Or surrender. It was difficult to tell which. After all, I had already learned from this biscuit what it had to teach me: that my first attempt could yield something edible, if not exceptional. I had seen where the recipe faltered, where my technique wavered. Was there truly anything to be gained by continuing?

But the thought of it—of letting the biscuit win—was intolerable. To place it in the trash would be to admit defeat, to acknowledge that it had bested me not through quality or grandeur, but through sheer, passive persistence. That was a victory I could not allow it.

I stepped back from the trash can and returned to the table, the biscuit waiting exactly where I had left it. Its plainness was unyielding, its lack of distinction as constant as the tide. And yet, I would finish it—not for its sake, but for mine.

I sat back down, and for a moment, the biscuit seemed... different. It hadn't been touched in my absence—of that I was certain—yet the time apart had altered the way I saw it. In leaving it unattended, I had allowed a sliver of doubt to creep in, as though my brief neglect had made it somehow less mine.

I leaned forward, studying it as one might study an old acquaintance after years apart, searching for any subtle change in posture or expression. Of course, the biscuit offered none. Its plainness was unchanged, its unassuming surface exactly as it had been before the phone rang. And yet, something in me felt the need to reassert my claim.

However unremarkable the biscuit may be, it was still my biscuit.

I picked it up, feeling again the familiar weight in my hand, the faint dryness against my fingertips. My resolve tightened. This was the next step toward finishing what I had started—toward eating this biscuit in its entirety, crumbs and all, and reclaiming the satisfaction that had been eroded by distractions.

I raised it slowly, the edge approaching my lips, the moment heavy with the quiet gravity of commitment. This was it. This was—

Knock knock.

The sound snapped the air like a twig underfoot.

I froze mid-motion, the biscuit suspended just shy of my mouth.

The knock at the door came again, softer this time, almost polite in its persistence. I set the biscuit down with a sigh that felt heavier than the moment warranted and went to answer.

On the other side stood a delivery driver, holding a slim cardboard box and a clipboard. A package. For me.

I couldn't remember ordering anything recently, but the man assured me it required my signature. This struck me as absurd—not the act of signing, but the idea that whatever was inside was so precious, so irreplaceable, that the possibility of it being stolen had to be guarded against with official acknowledgment. I scrawled my name with a pen that didn't quite work and accepted the box.

Back inside, I set it on the counter and opened it with the casual indifference of someone certain it would be nothing remarkable. I was correct. Inside were the thick wool socks I had ordered weeks ago in anticipation of the harsh winter the forecasts had promised—a winter which, if the weather channel's track record held true, would most likely be mild, uneventful, and as underwhelming as the biscuit waiting for me on the table.

These were not luxurious socks, not the sort that grace the feet of the wealthy in glossy magazine spreads. They were plain, functional, entirely ordinary. No one would covet them. No one would steal them. And yet, I had been made to sign for them, as though their loss would weigh heavily on my mind and my bank account. If they had been stolen—which I consider extraordinarily unlikely—I could have simply ordered another pair and thought nothing of it.

Instead, here they were. And there, on the table, was the biscuit, sitting in its smug plainness, mirroring the socks in spirit if not in form. Both unassuming. Both unremarkable. Neither bad nor particularly good. But at least the socks, in their modest way, promised to keep me warm.

I sat back down, the biscuit once again in hand, its

plain weight familiar against my fingers. I raised it toward my mouth and, just as my lips parted, a stray thought slid into my mind like a splinter: Did I ever...

The rest of the question was irrelevant. My body was already in motion, setting the biscuit back down as I stood to go check.

It was nothing urgent—in fact, it was barely worth the effort. A faint suspicion that I might have left the bathroom light on. Or that there was laundry still in the washer. Or perhaps—and I cannot say for certain—that the oven, cold and unused all day, somehow needed to be confirmed as off.

I wandered through the rooms, performing small, unnecessary acts of assurance, each one pulling me further from the kitchen. For a few minutes, the biscuit vanished from my awareness entirely, replaced by the small satisfactions of things tidied, checked, and put in their place.

Then, mid-step, it returned to me. The biscuit. Waiting. Still unfinished.

The thought landed with the strange gravity of a promise half-kept. I turned back toward the kitchen, feeling faintly as though I had abandoned an ally on the field. But this was no ally, no friendly comrade in arms waiting patiently for my return. No, this was a rather malignant biscuit—an enemy of greater proportion, simple and plain, mocking me repeatedly with its overt dryness.

The biscuit was exactly as I had left it, sitting motionless in the center of the plate, its surface unchanged, its expression unreadable—if a biscuit can be said to have an expression. And yet, something in its stillness felt heavier now.

This was no longer a "might as well" situation, no casual decision to eat simply because it was there. This was an act of principle.

The distractions had been many—the pointless phone call, the rogue crumb's expedition into the living room, the trash can's tempting call, the wool socks, signed-for with an air of undeserved formality, and the sudden wave of trivial tasks that had stolen my attention. Each had tried, in its own way, to derail me. And for a while, I had let them.

But not today.

I picked up the biscuit with a kind of ceremonial deliberation, feeling its familiar dryness against my fingertips. It had waited for me—not with loyalty, but with the smug patience of something confident it could outlast my will. It was wrong.

There would be no more delays, no more diversions. Whatever victories the biscuit had claimed in the form of scattered crumbs and stolen minutes, this final one would be mine.

It struck me, as I sat with the biscuit in hand, that distractions do more than steal time. Time, after all, can be regained in some form—shifted, rescheduled, borrowed from one moment to give to another. But momentum... momentum once broken is far harder to restore.

In the hours or days to come, I would forget this biscuit's exact taste. I would forget the number of bites it had taken to reach this point, or the precise sequence of events that had interrupted me. But I would remember the way each distraction had chipped away at the fragile resolve to finish what I had begun.

There is a particular danger in letting small things remain unfinished. The longer they sit, the heavier they become, until the weight of simply resuming is greater than the task itself. A single paused sentence can keep a writer from returning to the page for months. A neglected errand can loom so large that it becomes easier to ignore it entirely. Even something as simple as a biscuit, left untouched for too long, begins to feel like an obligation too daunting to complete.

I looked at it and felt the thought settle into place: If I cannot finish a biscuit without interruption, how can I expect to finish anything else?

The question was less about the biscuit now than it

was about myself. And yet, the biscuit remained the immediate test.

I resolved, quietly but completely, to finish it before anything else could pull me away again. Though I suspected—no, I knew—that the world, and perhaps the biscuit itself, would not make that task easy.

CHAPTER 7
The Last Bite

The plate was almost bare now, save for a single, solitary piece of biscuit. It sat slightly off-center, a small island of pale beige in an otherwise empty expanse of porcelain. This was it—the final remnant of what had once been whole, flanked now only by a scatter of crumbs that clung stubbornly to the plate's surface.

It was strange to think how much had happened to bring me here. How many pauses, how many diversions, how many philosophical tangents had been birthed in the time it took to work my way through this modest pastry. From the cautious optimism of the first bite, through the long plateau, the distractions, the crumbs' insurgency—all of it had funneled down to this: a mouthful.

There was a weight to it, not in the literal sense—it was lighter than it had any right to be—but in the fact that so much thought had been invested in its existence. For all the analysis, the asides, the digressions, and the moral debates, this was still, at its core, a piece of biscuit destined to be eaten.

And yet, in its smallness, it seemed to contain the sum of the entire experience.

I leaned in to study the final bite as if it might yet reveal some hidden truth. It was not, as I might have hoped, a perfect morsel—the kind one could imagine in a cookbook photograph, poised elegantly beside a steaming mug of tea. No, this was a slightly misshapen fragment, its edges irregular, one side bearing a thin crack where the crumb structure had given way under the pressure of earlier bites.

It seemed to hold more crumbs than substance, a fragile arrangement barely held together by the cohesion of what little moisture remained. A careless touch could reduce it to scattered fragments.

I turned it in my fingers, considering its fate. Should it be taken in one decisive motion, swallowed whole like a final line drawn under a long story? Or should it be savored—if that word could even be applied to something so persistently bland—in smaller nibbles, prolonging the end in the hope that some last, overlooked nuance might emerge?

The choice was absurd, and yet it held the weight of ceremony. It was not just a question of eating, but of how to close the chapter—with a swift conclusion, or a measured farewell.

It was light—almost offensively so. For all the time, thought, and effort that had been invested in reaching this point, the final bite weighed less than a coin, less than a folded scrap of paper. And yet, in my palm, it felt heavy in a way that had nothing to do with mass.

This was the last remnant of the biscuit—the final, tangible piece of something that had occupied my attention far longer than reason would ever justify. Its smallness seemed both fitting and disappointing. Fitting, because no ending ever truly matches the scale of its buildup; disappointing, because endings, however inevitable, carry with them a quiet hope of grandeur.

I rolled it slightly between my fingers, feeling its fragile give, its irregular edges. There was a strange duality to it—it was at once insignificant and important, trivial and symbolic, a nothing that somehow contained everything that had come before it.

And in that contradiction, I realized: this was not just the last bite of the biscuit. This was the last chance to alter my memory of it.

I held the last bite for a moment longer than necessary, letting the weight—or lack of it—settle into my hand. The room was still, save for the faint sound of my own breathing. There was no rush now. The end was close enough to touch, but far enough to linger over.

It reminded me of the first bite—that drawn-out pause before committing, the quiet inspection, the needless but somehow essential delay. Only this time, the anticipation carried no mystery. I knew exactly what awaited me. There would be no surprise, no sudden burst of hidden flavor, no revelation to alter the biscuit's legacy.

And yet, I hesitated all the same. Not because I expected more from it, but because the act of ending anything—no matter how small, no matter how plain—feels like closing a door you will not open again.

They say every ending is just another beginning—but not for the biscuit. For the biscuit, this was final. There would be no second life, no reincarnation, no return. Once gone, it would remain only as crumbs, memory, and perhaps a faint aftertaste that would fade before the plate was even cleared.

I took a breath and lowered it toward my mouth.

My teeth closed around the last bite with the slow precision of someone cataloging each sensation for the record. The crust—what little of it remained—gave the same modest resistance as before, fracturing without ceremony. The interior yielded easily, dry but not unpleasant, carrying the faintest ghost of butter across the tongue.

It was exactly as I remembered it. No better, no worse. No hidden depth revealed at the final moment, no triumphant swell of flavor as a parting gift. It was simply the biscuit, consistent to the end.

I chewed slowly, aware that these were the last seconds in which the biscuit would still exist in any meaningful form. The same quiet mediocrity that had defined it from the first bite to the last now carried me to the finish. And yet, there was something to be said for that constancy—for a thing that stayed what it was until the very end.

When I swallowed, it was with a faint sense of completion—nothing like elation, but unmistakably final. No victory fanfare played in my head, no rush of pride swelled in my chest. The satisfaction was quieter than that, simpler.

I did it!

The biscuit was gone.

And so it ended. The biscuit was gone—not dismantled, not abandoned, but consumed entirely, every intact piece claimed and accounted for. The long campaign that had stretched from the first tentative bite to this final, deliberate one had reached its conclusion.

Yet the victory was not complete. Across the plate, the table, my shirt, and—somewhere—the living room couch, the biscuit's scattered army remained. The crumbs lay in quiet defiance, holding their positions as if to remind me that even in defeat, the biscuit had managed to leave its mark.

The battle for the biscuit was over. The battle with its remains was yet to come.

CHAPTER 8

Victory, Momentum, and the Mess Ahead

The plate was empty. Completely, gloriously empty. Where once there had been a biscuit—plain, unremarkable, stubbornly persistent—there remained only the faint dusting of its remains and the pale ring left behind where it had rested.

I could still taste it faintly, a ghost of its last crumb clinging to my tongue. The dryness lingered too, the kind that asks for a sip of something but can just as easily be ignored in favor of the moment's purity. A few stubborn flecks clung to my fingertips, as if reluctant to let me go, and I brushed them idly against my palm.

For a moment, I allowed myself to bask in it. The absence of it felt as full as the presence it once had—a curious fullness, not of stomach but of spirit. I had done what I set out to do. Bite by bite, pause by pause, distraction by distraction, I had seen it through to the end.

And yes, I was aware of the absurdity. Standing triumphant over the empty plate as if I had conquered something monumental. I might have laughed at myself if I weren't so busy enjoying the ridiculous grandeur of it all.

It was a small thing, perhaps even an absurd thing, but it was mine. My biscuit. My victory.

I had done it. I had begun, persevered, and finished. The journey from first bite to last had not been swift, nor without obstacle, but it was now complete. And in that completion, I felt something stir—a renewed conviction, a momentum I had not felt in... well, longer than I cared to admit.

This was not just the end of a biscuit. This was proof.

Proof that I could see a thing through from start to finish, regardless of its trials, its tedium, or its plainness. For too long, I had let projects linger unfinished: half-read books, half-built models, ideas started with zeal only to be abandoned in the quiet drag of the middle. But no longer. The biscuit had changed me.

If I could finish this—this biscuit—then what could possibly stand in my way? There was no task too great, no undertaking too ambitious. I would return to the projects gathering dust on shelves. I would write the words left unwritten. I would fix the drawer that had been sticking for three years. I could repaint the hallway, finally pair all the socks in the drawer, perhaps even learn Mandarin— because I had proven, here and now, that I could do what I started.

Some might scoff at the significance I placed on such a small victory. Let them. They had not fought this battle. They had not stared down the monotony, the distractions, the slow creep of crumb insurgency, and emerged victorious. The biscuit had been my Everest— modest in size, yes, but towering in the quiet demands it made of my patience and persistence. And with the final bite, I had planted my flag in its summit's snow.

The plate before me was the summit. From its broad white expanse, I could see everything—the pale ring where the biscuit once lay, the faint golden dust that clung stubbornly to its surface, the unbroken horizon of emptiness stretching out in all directions. It was not so different, I imagined, from standing atop Everest: the air thin with triumph, the heart pounding with the exertion of the climb, the world spread out beneath me in a panorama so vast and clear that it silenced thought. True, there were no mountain ranges, no glaciers shimmering in the sun—but the plate had its own stark beauty, a minimalism earned through struggle.

Yet even from this lofty vantage, I could see what waited below. The battlefield stretched outward from the plate's edge: clusters of crumbs huddled in defensive formation on the table's surface, a scattering of larger fragments lying where they had fallen, each a casualty of the final bites. On my shirt, more survivors clung defiantly, lodged in the folds of my lap like guerrilla fighters. Somewhere in the living room, a rogue outpost had established itself. And in the couch's seams, no doubt, entire crumb legions lay in silent ambush, awaiting some future archaeologist to uncover their remains and speculate on the mysterious biscuit-based civilization that once flourished here.

Still, I reminded myself—the summit had been reached. The flag had been planted with the final bite, and though the wind might carry whispers of unfinished work, the victory was real. One could stand in triumph and still acknowledge the road ahead.

I had won the war, but the battlefield still needed clearing.

It was strange, really—to sit here feeling the quiet satisfaction of victory while surrounded by the evidence of an unfinished task. The biscuit was gone, yet it still occupied the room in its scattered remains.

I couldn't help but smile at the irony. All my grand declarations, all my talk of perseverance and momentum, and here I was hesitating to sweep a few crumbs into my hand. The battle had proven my will; the cleanup would prove my follow-through—and that was a trial I found myself in no rush to face.

If eating the biscuit had been my Everest, then the climb down loomed before me now: treacherous terrain of tabletop and shirtfront, each crumb a loose stone conspiring to send me tumbling back into apathy. Gravity is never so persistent as when you're trying to get home. And so I sat, letting the victory linger, already suspecting this descent might be delayed until... another day.

CHAPTER 9
Post-Biscuit Silence

No crumbs. No smears. No lingering fragments of defiance. Just a smooth, white surface, reflecting the muted light of the room like a freshly wiped slate.

And yet, the silence that followed was not the absence of sound—the hum of the fridge still buzzed faintly in the background, a car murmured past outside, the occasional tick of the wall clock persisted in its stubborn rhythm. No, this silence was of a different kind. A hush not of the world, but of the self.

The room hadn't grown quieter.

I had.

There's a peculiar stillness that arrives after completion—not triumph, not relief, but a kind of internal decrescendo. Like some part of me that had been holding its breath through the entire ordeal was finally allowed to exhale. The tension didn't snap or shatter or release in dramatic flourish. It simply faded.

I stared at the plate for a while. Too long, maybe. But I wasn't ready to move. Not yet. Because for all its plainness, all its relentless mediocrity, that biscuit had become... something. A focal point. A task. A symbol, even if I didn't ask for one.

And now that it was gone, I was no longer tethered to its slow, dry gravity. I was floating. Not upwards, not into glory—just slightly adrift. Just... untethered.

I hadn't realized how much space the biscuit had taken up—not on the plate, not in the kitchen, but in my mind.

And with its absence, a gentle, curious void was left behind.

My mouth felt... dry.

Not parched—nothing dramatic. Just that faint, papery dryness that clings to the inside of the cheeks when starch has overstayed its welcome. The kind of dryness that whispers, rather than shouts, for water. But I didn't move. Not yet. There was something oddly fitting about letting the biscuit have the final say, even if it was through the terrain it had left behind.

There was a trace of salt still lingering on my tongue, like the ghost of flavor too subtle to be called taste. Not enough to savor. Not enough to forget, either. A flavorless echo. The kind that lingers not because it was bold, but because it never quite resolved into anything distinct. It just stayed.

I ran my tongue over my teeth—and found it. A single crumb. Lodged, stubbornly, between molars.

Of course.

It wasn't sharp, nor irritating. It didn't demand floss or vengeance. It was simply... there. Uninvited, but not wholly unexpected. A parting gift from a biscuit that refused to vanish entirely, even in defeat. A reminder that victory over a biscuit is never absolute. Not truly.

I considered retrieving it right away—to reclaim the sanctity of a clean mouth—but something in me hesitated. That crumb, in all its insolence, had earned its moment. Let it rest there a little longer, like the final ember of a fire too stubborn to die out.

The biscuit was gone. And yet, it wasn't.

The biscuit was gone. Not a trace on the plate. Not a purpose left in front of me.

And yet, I still sat there, as if my body hadn't received the message. My posture hadn't changed. My hands still hovered faintly above the table, uncertain of what to do now that they were no longer tasked with holding, cradling, defending a singular, unremarkable bite.

There was a weight missing—not on the plate, but in me.

Not grief, exactly. Not loss. More like... a sudden decompression. The quiet, disorienting sensation of realizing you've been holding your breath without noticing, and now you don't need to. A subtle kind of unmooring. I hadn't been waiting for this moment, and yet its arrival had removed a purpose I hadn't meant to give it.

I looked at the plate again, trying to feel triumphant. But triumph had no interest in this kind of victory. What I felt instead was space. A small, curious space where a biscuit used to be.

It hadn't earned that space by being remarkable. It had simply existed long enough in my mind—persisted through distractions, survived my doubts, outlasted temptations to throw it away—that its absence now rang louder than its presence ever had.

And there it was, that simple truth:

"The end of something small can still leave a space."

The silence had texture now.

Not the oppressive kind that fills a room after an argument, nor the soothing quiet of a peaceful morning. This was a neutral silence. A silence that simply... existed. It didn't care what I did next. It didn't press, or comfort, or judge. It just was.

And I sat in it. Not doing. Not thinking. Just... being.

The plate remained in front of me—empty, expectant. Crumbs clung stubbornly to its edges, some scattered across the table like the final thoughts of a dream already fading. A small battlefield, not yet cleared.

There was a calm detachment now, a peculiar stillness in my mind. The biscuit was finished. The saga, ridiculous as it had been, had played itself out. And yet, the room hadn't declared a victor. There was no fanfare, no applause. Only the quiet knowing that something had ended.

And maybe—just maybe—that meant something else could begin.

I could clean up. I could stare at the crumbs and reflect some more. I could even, in a moment of unchecked madness... bake again.

That last thought lingered longer than I expected.

Not because I wanted to relive the experience, but because something in me needed to understand it. What had gone so... right? Or wrong? What alchemy of mismeasured ingredients and misplaced expectations had led to such perfect mediocrity?

A biscuit so plainly itself that it defied comment. Not bad. Not good. Just... biscuit.

No, if I was ever to bake again—and who's to say I wouldn't—I'd need to return to the beginning. To revisit the quiet chaos behind the recipe. The triumphs. The failures. The moment I stood at the precipice of creation and dared to whisper, "Yes. A biscuit."

But for now, there was only the silence.

Not unpleasant. Not comforting.

Just silence.

Silence as plain and unremarkable as the biscuit itself. A silence with no dramatic hush, no sacred stillness, just the auditory equivalent of beige. No, this silence was flavorless in emotion, crumbly in purpose, and yet undeniably present. Not golden like a fresh loaf, nor hearty like a crusted roll—just meek, beige, and barely worth mentioning.

A silence born not of bread, but of biscuit—a silence that sits in the soul like a dry mouthful of unfinished thoughts.

Dry, simple, undemanding... and somehow still lingering.

CHAPTER 10
Too Late for Butter

It was gone now. The biscuit. Consumed, digested, rendered into whatever mundane destiny awaits all baked goods after ingestion. There were no fireworks, no sudden spiritual clarity, no applause from the universe. Just silence... and the faint, familiar dryness still haunting the edges of my teeth.

I had eaten it.

And yet, even now, in this aftermath, I found myself circling it—not with teeth or hands, but with thought. So much thought. Far too much thought, really. The kind of thought one might reserve for a lover lost too soon, or a life decision that split time into a Before and an After.

Instead, mine had been a biscuit. A plain, dry biscuit of my own making.

Not a bad biscuit, no—let's not be unfair. But certainly not a good one. The kind of biscuit that, when gone, leaves not a memory but a shrug. A sigh. A faint salivary confusion.

And yet here I was, hours—perhaps days, perhaps mere moments; time had grown soft around the edges—still thinking about it. Replaying the act of eating it with the scrutiny of an art critic dissecting a still life painting of beige food on a beige plate in a beige gallery curated by beige people.

Why?

That question lingered like the taste had—faint, unimportant, but somehow persistent.

Was it the biscuit's fault? Or mine? Had I imbued it with too much weight from the beginning, built up its importance until the act of eating it became a minor epic? Or had I, in fact, not given it enough importance when it mattered most—when it could have been saved, uplifted, transformed with even the smallest of condiments?

Butter.

Jam.

Honey.

Gravy, even.

Each option now floated in my mind like ghosts of flavor never realized, echoes of choices unchosen. I had not simply eaten a biscuit. I had eaten the wrong version of a biscuit—a version that could have, with a single addition, meant something more.

And now it was too late.

Too late for butter.

Too late for jam.

Too late, even, for regret to feel fresh.

But not too late to think about it. Oh no, the thinking had only just begun.

If I had added honey—just honey—would everything have been different?

Not a flood. Not a cascade. Just the faintest curl of golden syrup drawn across the biscuit's plain surface, like the sun deciding to linger just a little longer on the edge of an otherwise gray morning. A touch of amber gloss where once there was only matte disappointment.

It's easy, now, to imagine it:

The honey glinting in the light, thick and slow, stretching like a sigh before finally surrendering to gravity.

The spoon twisting above the biscuit like a painter over canvas, waiting for just the right moment, the right motion, to make meaning.

The biscuit, once dry and forgettable, now catching the light like it mattered.

But that is the temptation of honey—it is not a condiment, it is a fantasy. A glistening indulgence whose sweetness is almost too perfect to trust. It plays at generosity while knowing it will vanish the moment it touches your tongue. Ephemeral. Addictive. Gentle deception in viscous form.

And yet...

Wouldn't it have made the dryness easier? Wouldn't the contrast—the subtle bitterness of baked flour and salt, met by the soft kiss of sugar—have turned the moment into something... real?

Even the imagined pairing was enough to make my molars tingle in phantom delight.

Perhaps the biscuit would have soaked it just enough to soften its resistance, but not so much as to dissolve its integrity. The crumb would remain, but humbled. The dryness, less insult than character.

Of course, in the dream, I see the honey behaving.

But in reality?

It drips too fast. It runs, not drizzles. It pools. Suddenly the plate is a sticky battlefield and the biscuit is soggy on one edge and untouched on the other. It dares me to balance flavor and form, to judge speed against saturation. The micro-drama plays out in full.

And that's not even addressing the real crisis: which honey?

Do I reach for the raw, unfiltered kind, thick with sediment and comb—rustic, defiant, a product of bees who live on the edges of society and forage in the bitter fields of self-reliance?

Or do I opt for the cheerful plastic bear from the supermarket shelf—familiar, bright, and arguably not honey at all, but a golden lie packaged for convenience?

Perhaps a regional specialty. Manuka, with its medicinal tang. Wildflower, with its chaotic floral blur. Clover, the safe option—a median sweetness for a median biscuit.

Each choice a statement. Each option a reflection of who I am... or who I want to be.

Filtered or unfiltered? Local or imported? Viscous or thin?

Budget or boutique?

Am I the kind of person who pairs mediocrity with

ambition, or one who insists that a plain biscuit deserves only a plain adornment?

No answer came. Only more options.

More questions.

And in the silence of all that imagined sweetness...

...I tasted nothing.

Because I had eaten the biscuit.

Without honey.

And now all that remained was thought.

Butter.

Even the word itself melts on the tongue—two soft syllables that linger without urgency. Not like jam with its jolt of consonants, nor honey with its syrupy optimism. No, butter is quieter. Humble. Heavier. More grounded.

I imagine it now: the pale yellow slab resting on the counter, catching the morning light just so. A glisten here. A curl of waxed paper peeled back like a gift slowly unwrapped.

Not melted—not yet—but pliant. Soft enough to yield to the blade without resistance, firm enough to keep its shape under pressure. Effort met with grace.

And the knife—

a small press, a gentle pull, and the edge glides through with a satisfying drag, leaving behind a perfect ridge of promise.

That first swipe across the biscuit's surface—warm enough to coax transformation, cool enough to delay it. The butter doesn't sit on the biscuit; it becomes part of it. It sinks in, disappears slowly into the waiting crumb, as if whispering:

"I was always meant to be here."

I imagine the warmth of the biscuit, modest though it was, inviting the butter to dance. A slow-motion waltz of fat and starch, gleaming slightly, releasing a fragrance that's somehow both rich and simple. A smell that could haunt kitchens and memory alike.

The dryness? Gone.

The neutrality? Transcended.

The biscuit? Elevated.

A peasant, now dressed for court.

And here's the strange thing—it isn't just taste.

Butter is transformation.

It is the quiet metaphor of life's simplest effort made manifest.

A meager act—one spread, one gesture—and the entire experience shifts. It asks almost nothing, yet offers everything in return. It's not loud. It's not demanding.

But it is kind.

Or... it could have been.

Because then—of course—the questions begin.

Salted or unsalted?

Salted butter brings character. Confidence. It speaks for itself and, if you're not careful, for the entire dish. But unsalted? Unsalted is pure potential—quiet, deferent, a blank page on which flavor might be written... or forgotten entirely.

And what of cultured butter? That touch of tang, that complexity born of time and intention. A butter that has lived. A butter that has seen things.

Am I that kind of person? The kind who reaches for culture—for depth, for fermentation, for a little edible mystery?

Or do I spread margarine, that imposter, that yellow compromise pretending to be more than chemistry?

No cows. No cream. Just... oil. Hope. And artificial yellow number five.

Is choosing margarine a betrayal of the biscuit? Or a realistic nod to cholesterol?

And how much?

A sliver? A pat?

An elegant sheen across the top?

Or a ruinous heap of dairy excess, slathered so thickly that the biscuit becomes secondary—a mere vessel, a butter delivery system, an edible napkin?

What of fresh-churned? The poetry of hand-labored cream in a rustic jar, shaken into glory with sweat and dedication?

Too quaint, perhaps. Too aspirational.

And store-bought?

Accessible, predictable, disappointingly square.

There are even ethical implications. Grass-fed or grain-fed cows? Local dairy or global supply chain?

What began as indulgence now stands trial.

Flavor has become philosophy.

And so, I'm left sitting here, the biscuit long gone, but the butter—the idea of butter—tormenting me with its infinite variables.

A thousand potential outcomes.

A thousand slightly softened, slightly salted realities.

Each one real enough to taste.

None of them mine.

Jam.

Now here is no modest enhancement—this is declaration. Where butter whispers, jam sings. Bold. Bright. Unapologetically vibrant. A smear of color across the pale page of the biscuit.

I picture it—a deep red swirl of strawberry or perhaps the purple glisten of blackberry. The sort of spread that leaves traces not only on the crumb but on fingers, napkins, and, somehow, the soul.

There is something ceremonial about opening a jar of jam—the pop of the lid, the faint mist of preserved sweetness that escapes. It smells like summer. Like breakfasts never quite achieved. Like possibilities.

And the seeds—always the seeds. Tiny interruptions that catch in the teeth, reminders that even joy can be inconvenient. But they're proof, aren't they? Proof that the fruit was real. That it once hung from a branch, basked in the sun, ripened naturally before being crushed into something edible and metaphorical.

Imagine the contrast: the biscuit's dry neutrality, meeting the vivid burst of sugared fruit.

It's not just taste—it's opposition.

The sweetness and the tartness, the bright acidity clashing gently with the beige monotony. It's the balance of opposites. Joy against plainness.

Life against sustenance.

It might have been perfect.

If —

And that's always the word, isn't it?

If I had chosen jam.

If I had chosen the right jam.

Because the spiral begins here—this is no longer about enhancement, but identity.

Strawberry? Safe. Familiar. Nostalgic. The jam of childhood toast and simple joys. But... does it lack ambition?

Raspberry? Elegant. Tart. Seeds like little punctuation marks. Bold, yet occasionally smug.

Blackberry? Earthy. Rich. The jam of forest picnics and thorny fingers. But those seeds... those seeds are an invasion.

Apricot? Delightfully tangy, golden like sunlit afternoons. But prone to over-sweetness.

Fig? Mysterious. Exotic. The choice of someone with a cheese board and opinions on balsamic vinegar.

Marmalade? Bitter. Sophisticated. A jam that dares you to grow up.

Quince? Is that even jam, or some mythical preserve whispered about by food bloggers?

And what of texture?

Do I want smooth? Chunky? Preserves or jelly?

Am I trying to taste fruit or merely remember it?

There's also the contextual crisis:

Do I crave the jam of my youth? The plastic squeeze bottle of processed joy, artificial and utterly sincere?

Or do I reach for the artisanal jar I once bought at a farmer's market for eight dollars and promptly forgot in the back of the fridge until it became an ecosystem?

Even availability plays its part.

Perhaps I had no jam at all.

Or worse—I had one jar, half-used, whose label had worn off. A jam without identity. A jam of doubt.

And how would it have spread?

Too thick? It tears the biscuit.

Too thin? It seeps into the crumb, disappears without a trace.

Worse still—the uneven spread.

One quadrant coated in fruity splendor, the other left naked.

Every bite a gamble.

Each mouthful a moral failing.

And what if—no, this is unbearable—what if the jam clashed with the biscuit?

What if the biscuit, for all its plainness, had opinions?

What if the pairing was wrong—like two polite acquaintances forced into conversation at a wedding?

No, it's too much.

Jam is not a condiment. It is a commitment.

A statement of who I am, what I want, and what I fear.

So I sat there, jamless.

Because the moment had passed.

Because the decision was too heavy.

Because somewhere in the pantry of my soul, the jam shelf had collapsed.

And then came the flood.

For if not honey, and not butter, and not jam... then what?

What else might have lifted the biscuit from its culinary purgatory?

Gravy?

A savory rebellion. Bold. Moist. A complete betrayal of the biscuit's sweet potential—but perhaps that's what it needed. A smothering. A rescue. A second chance drowned in peppered redemption.

Clotted cream?

Decadence incarnate. The kind of topping whispered about in tea rooms, served with silver spoons and class-based anxiety. Thick, soft, and vaguely unsettling in name—but oh, the way it would rest atop the crumb like royalty on a modest throne.

Cheese?

A curious curveball. Sharp cheddar? Brie? A blue so bold it offends the senses? Biscuit and cheese—a love story no one asked for, but some believe in.

It would have been unorthodox. Risky. Possibly genius.

Possibly a mistake worthy of exile.

Peanut butter?

Nostalgic. Protein-rich. Overpowering.

A spread that turns every bite into a workout.

Would it stick to the roof of my mouth? Yes.

Would it dry me out further? Absolutely.

Would it have made the biscuit better?

That depends on whether I wanted a snack... or a challenge.

Maple syrup?

Liquid gold. Unpredictable. Uncontainable.

The topping that doesn't spread so much as wander, pooling in corners of the plate like a rebel with a sugar high.

It would sweeten the biscuit, yes—but at what cost to structure? To dignity?

Mustard?

Why?

No.

And yet...?

Yogurt. Hummus. Nutella. Apple butter. Aioli. Salsa. Whipped cream. Pesto. Marmite. Marshmallow fluff.

A dozen more contenders flash through my mind like contestants in a reality show I never agreed to judge.

Each offering transformation. Each demanding attention.

Each carrying its own risks, its own regrets.

It is no longer a question of improvement.

It is a question of identity.

What kind of biscuit do I want this to be?

What kind of person am I to have allowed it to remain so bare?

I thought having choices would empower me.

But now, the options pile like unopened mail—each one a reminder of something undone.

Too many roads.

Too many forks.

Too many spoons.

And yet, no single answer feels right.

Or rather, too many answers feel right enough.

I begin to suspect that perhaps...

Perhaps the problem was never the toppings.

Perhaps the real issue... was me.

Or worse:

The biscuit was already exactly what it was meant to be.

In the end, I did not add anything.

No honey, no butter, no jam. Not even a desperate dab of gravy or an impulsive smear of cheese.

The biscuit entered this world plain and dry—and so it left it.

Perhaps... that was always its fate.

A biscuit that promises nothing is, at the very least, honest. It cannot disappoint you with false sweetness or betray you with unexpected salt. It simply is, and asks nothing more than to be acknowledged, perhaps consumed. Its humility is its truth.

Its blandness... its creed.

I think now of all the options. The symphony of spreads. The orchestra of possible toppings.

And yet none were chosen. None were right.

Or worse... they were all too right, and therefore none could be.

They say anticipation heightens the pleasure.

Perhaps it does. But in the case of this biscuit...

Well...

I suspect the anticipation was the only pleasure to be had.

The first bite was never about flavor.

It was about hope.

And so I sat there, staring at the empty plate, and I whispered to myself a truth I dared not say aloud: "In hindsight, perhaps eating it plain and dry was not the best idea."

...But then again... perhaps that was the point.

Because the failure was never in the toppings I didn't add.

The failure—if one dares to use such a strong word—was baked in long before the biscuit ever met the plate.

Which leaves only one course of action.

If I am to understand this biscuit—truly understand why it became what it became—then I must go back.

Not to the toppings.

Not to the moment of the bite.

But to the mixing.

To the measuring.

To the sacred and perhaps misguided rituals that gave it life.

If there is meaning in the crumb, I will find it.

If there is redemption in the bake, I will seek it.

And if not...

Well, then I'll just make another biscuit.

But better this time.

Maybe.

Perhaps.

Probably not.

PART TWO

BEHIND THE BISCUIT

CHAPTER 11
The Hunger That Began It All

It didn't hit like a pang or strike like a craving. No gnawing in the gut. No sharp reminder of skipped meals or missed snacks. Just... something.

A soft emptiness.

It began as a shift in posture—the kind you make when something internal feels slightly off. Not quite discomfort, but not quite peace either. A slow awareness of absence. A whisper from within saying, "You should... maybe... eat?" But even that suggestion arrived uncertain, as if unwilling to commit to being a need.

I sat with it for a while, hoping it would define itself. Sometimes thirst masquerades as hunger. Sometimes it's boredom wearing a salt craving's mask. Sometimes you're just tired and your body throws ideas at you like darts, hoping one will stick. And sometimes, though rarely spoken aloud, hunger is not for sustenance at all.

Sometimes, it's just longing—vague, rootless, unnameable. A craving not of the stomach, but of the soul.

I shifted again.

Was I hungry for food... or for something else pretending to be food?

An answer didn't come. Only that quiet ache persisted, soft and ambiguous. Like a half-remembered name on the tip of your tongue, or a melody hummed by someone you don't know but swear you've heard before.

Whatever it was, it would not resolve itself by thought alone.

Eventually, I stood. Not because I knew what I wanted, but because I was tired of wondering.

I rose not with purpose, but with a kind of quiet resignation—the way you might rise to greet a neighbor you barely know who's knocked at your door for no clear reason. A politeness toward the self, perhaps.

The fridge was the first stop, as it often is—the cold confessional booth of indecision. I opened it slowly, as if doing so gently might change the contents. It did not.

A half-used tub of cream cheese. A leftover something—probably edible. A jar of pickles with three survivors floating like forgotten thoughts. A lonely carrot. Cold light poured over it all, sterile and judgmental.

Nothing jumped out. Not literally—though I half-expected it—nor metaphorically. These were ingredients, not meals. A collection of maybes requiring action. Preparation. Work. I was not hungry for work.

I closed the fridge with the kind of pause that makes the act feel profound, as though I were sealing away a chapter of my life. I wasn't. I was just stalling.

To the pantry.

Its hinges sighed as if they, too, were tired of me. Shelves lined with boxes, bags, and jars—a catalog of promises, none fulfilled. Cans that demanded heating. Pastas that begged for sauce. Rice that needed rinsing, measuring, watching.

Potential. Endless, exhausting potential.

What I wanted wasn't a project. It wasn't something to make or build or craft. I didn't want to measure. I didn't want to season. I didn't want to wonder if I had basil. I wanted completion. I wanted conclusion. Something I could consume without narrative or prep time.

"I wasn't hungry for effort," I admitted aloud to no one.

"I was hungry for resolution."

But resolution, it seemed, was not shelved conveniently between the peanut butter and the stale crackers.

I drifted, not quite walking, not quite pacing—more of a shuffle guided by quiet dissatisfaction and the hope that motion might shake loose an idea. The pantry had offered nothing but potential. The fridge, only disappointment chilled to regulation temperature. The counter? No help. The table? Empty. The fruit bowl? A tragic lie.

I circled back through the kitchen and peeked into the living room as if perhaps, by miracle, there'd be something snackable on the coffee table. There wasn't, unless I'd suddenly developed a craving for coasters or remote controls.

I returned to the kitchen, defeated but still upright. That was something.

I opened a cupboard at random. Cereal—too sweet. I opened a drawer. Trail mix—too ambitious. I stared at the jar of peanut butter. Too sticky. The crackers? Too dry. The chips? Too noisy. The yogurt? Too cold and far too smug.

Everything had a flaw. Everything had... a personality. Opinions, textures, extremes. Loud flavors, loud packaging, loud consequences.

What I needed was something that did not demand an opinion. Something that didn't assault the senses with obligation. I didn't want something decadent. I didn't want something disgusting. I wanted... a presence. A vessel. A moment of edible neutrality.

That's when the thought arrived—soft, subtle, and mostly subconscious:

A biscuit.

Not the grand, flaky sort they serve with gravy and apologies in Southern diners. No. Not the sweet British kind either, which are really just cookies with an accent. I meant a plain, humble, undeniably beige biscuit. The kind that isn't trying to be anything more than it is. A baked shrug. A culinary ellipsis.

I had always wanted to learn how to make a good biscuit. Not because biscuits are impressive—they aren't. But because they are honest. They are simple yet elegant. Tasteful yet basic. They do not lie.

And that—at last—felt like a start.

It wasn't a lightning bolt. There was no crescendo of

music, no whisper from the heavens, no memory-laced epiphany from my childhood involving flour-dusted countertops and grandmotherly smiles.

No, it was simpler than that.

I didn't choose the biscuit.

I merely allowed the idea of it to go unchallenged.

The thought had arrived—soft and vague—and I hadn't the energy to argue with it. It was not the best option. It wasn't even a particularly good one. It was, at best, not worse than the rest.

Everything else required something of me. Flavor, judgment, cleanup, consequence. But a biscuit? A biscuit was a manageable disappointment.

And in that moment, that was enough.

I let the word settle. Biscuit. Not shouted, not sung. Just spoken internally with the same tone one might use to acknowledge the weather. A nod of recognition. A shrug of the soul.

Yes.

A biscuit.

That will do.

CHAPTER 12

The Fridge, the Pantry, and the Graveyard of Options

I paced. Not briskly—not in the manner of someone preparing for an undertaking of great importance—but with the sluggish indecision of someone who had agreed to a commitment they didn't fully understand.

A biscuit.

At the time, it had seemed so reasonable. Modest. Comforting, even. A humble answer to a humble question.

But now, standing in the too-still air of the kitchen, I began to suspect that I had made a terrible mistake.

A biscuit is not, as it turns out, a simple thing. It is flour and fat and a leavening agent. It is measuring, mixing, cutting, baking. It is time. It is effort. And worst of all—worst of all—it is cleanup. Dishes, flour on the counter, butter where butter ought not be. This was not a snack. This was a culinary detour.

And for what? A disc of edible disappointment?

I ran a hand through my hair and muttered aloud:

"Surely, there must be something simpler."

It wasn't a cry of desperation. Not yet. But it was close. The kind of plea whispered by someone on the edge of pouring cereal and pretending that counts as dinner. The kind of whisper that hopes—irrationally, foolishly—that maybe, just maybe, the fridge has refilled itself in the last five minutes. Maybe the pantry has rearranged its contents into something inspiring.

I stopped pacing. Turned toward the cold glow of the refrigerator like a pilgrim toward the shrine. My shoulders sagged with the weight of hope I did not want to carry.

One more look. One more survey of the barren

possibilities.

Not because I no longer wanted a biscuit.

But because now that I did—I desperately wished I didn't.

I opened the fridge the way one might open a long-forgotten treasure chest—slowly, reverently, and with a disproportionate amount of hope.

The light flickered to life with a hum that sounded vaguely disappointed.

First: the half-used tub of cream cheese. Its lid was askew, as if even it had given up. The edges had crusted over into a rind-like border, encircling the vaguely glossy smear at its center. It looked like it had once been involved in something meaningful—a bagel, perhaps—but had since been abandoned to its fate, a spread without a cause. It was not so much unappetizing as it was deeply untrustworthy.

Next, the leftover something. It sat in a container so clouded with fridge-fog and clingy regret that any attempt to identify its contents would have required a degree in speculative forensics. It was beige-ish. Or maybe gray. Or perhaps that was the lighting. It was probably edible—in the same way that most things technically are—but it carried the heavy weight of ambiguity. The kind of food that inspires not hunger but philosophical questions. Who made this? When? Why?

Then, the jar of pickles—or more accurately, the three survivors floating in a briny purgatory. They bobbed like confused old men in a communal bath, unsure if they were relaxing or dissolving. The jar had clearly been full once. Now, it was mostly pickle-essence and disappointment. I considered eating one, briefly. Just to say I had eaten something. But it felt too desperate, too performative. Pickles should never be eaten out of spite.

Ah yes. And the carrot.

Just the one.

Lonely, slightly bendy, with a faint white blush forming where it had begun to dry. It wasn't rotten—

not exactly. But it had passed the point of ideal crunch and entered that tragic twilight between raw snack and compost. I could eat it, sure. If I hated myself.

I scanned again. Shelf by shelf. Bottles and jars of sauces whose purposes I had long forgotten. A mustard too fancy to throw away, too strong to enjoy. A salsa that was mostly liquid. An unopened container of plain yogurt that somehow expired two weeks ago despite being brand new. And always—always—that deceptively cheerful tub of hummus, eternally perched near the front, inviting and unwanted.

I closed the fridge with a slow sigh.

Nothing had changed.

Nothing had been gained.

Only now, my hope was colder.

Back to the pantry.

Its hinges sighed as if they, too, were tired of me. Perhaps even ashamed—opening once more for a seeker who would almost certainly leave unfulfilled.

Inside: shelves lined with boxes, bags, and jars. A catalog of promises, none fulfilled. An archive of intentions. Food in the abstract.

There were beans—dried, of course. Always dried. The kind that required soaking, boiling, seasoning, patience. The kind that whispered, "I could nourish you... if only you gave me eight hours and a bay leaf." I did not have a bay leaf. I barely had eight minutes.

Next, rice. A 10-pound sack of it—smug in its abundance. So versatile, so essential, so aggressively neutral. But it wanted too much. It wanted rinsing. Measuring. Watching. It wanted attention. It was the kind of food that needed to be seen, cared for. I wasn't in the mood for that kind of relationship.

Oats. Plain rolled oats, in a giant cardboard cylinder that seemed to exist in every pantry, always partially used, never empty, never replaced. They sat there like a dusty sentinel of healthful decisions never made. I stared at them. They stared back. Neither of us blinked.

Flour. Sugar. Baking soda. Vanilla extract. Yeast.

Cinnamon. Everything one might need to bake something glorious. Everything one might need to fail at baking something glorious.

I picked up a box of pasta. Penne, I think. Or ziti. One of those shapes that tries to have an identity but ultimately just exists to be covered in sauce and forgotten. But I had no sauce. Not even canned tomatoes. Just the pasta—a blank canvas with no artist in sight.

There were canned goods—corn, green beans, a lone tin of tuna. Food that had long since given up the idea of being inspiring. They were there for emergencies, not moments of clarity. They existed to not be eaten.

And so many bags. Bags of lentils. Of quinoa. Of things that sounded virtuous but felt emotionally distant. Superfoods with superiority complexes.

There was potential, yes. But potential is not dinner. Potential is not comfort.

Potential is exhausting.

What I wanted wasn't a challenge or an opportunity for growth. I didn't want a project. I wanted a result. Something I could hold in my hand, put in my mouth, and be done with. Something finished, or at the very least—finishable.

And yet, as I gently closed the pantry door, I felt it: a faint twinge of guilt. These were good ingredients. Honest ingredients. Hardworking, foundational elements of civilization itself.

But today... today I had no desire to build a civilization.

I returned to the fridge.

Perhaps, I thought, the third time's the charm. Or perhaps—as with so many things in life—repetition does not yield reward, only awareness.

It greeted me with the same chill, though somehow the cold felt more personal this time. Less like refrigeration and more like judgment.

The light flickered on with a weary hum, as if to say, "You again?"

Everything was still exactly where I had left it. And

yet... something had shifted. Not in the fridge. In me.

"Perhaps the act of looking alters the seer, not the seen." A thought that felt profound for half a second before I remembered I was standing barefoot in front of a fridge, contemplating pickles.

And there they were—the pickles—still adrift in their cloudy brine like ancient relics in a museum display. The final three survivors. Less a snack, more a warning.

I stared at them. They stared back.

One tilted slightly, as if raising an eyebrow.

I shut the door slowly.

Not angrily. Not hastily. But like one ends a conversation that has gone on too long with someone who is both boring and slightly condescending.

There were no answers in the fridge.

Just... continuity.

The cupboards had waited patiently.

If the fridge was the cold shoulder of the kitchen, the cupboards were its long-lost memory—dusty, neglected, and filled with objects that once promised joy but now whispered only "someday."

I opened one. Not the usual one. One in the back—high up, slightly swollen from humidity, the kind that requires a stretch and a silent negotiation with gravity.

Inside, it was a time capsule.

There it was: The Snack That Time Forgot—a once-beloved granola bar, now a relic. The wrapper faded, crinkled like parchment. I dared not check the expiration date. I was certain it had crossed into another era.

Behind it: The Pasta of Prophecy. A half-used bag of noodles, its twist-tie long gone, the top folded in a desperate accordion of hope. The contents rattled like bones. I considered whether this pasta might appear in my next dream to warn me of impending doom.

Then, in the darkest corner, a tin of something unmarked—a can so generic it defied branding. Smooth label. No text. No image. A riddle in aluminum. I held it in my hand like an artifact from an unknown civilization. I returned it just as reverently.

Drawer after drawer, cupboard after cupboard—each yielded nothing but tales. A jar of peanut butter, half-empty and wholly sticky. A collection of mismatched teas, all promising exotic awakenings but delivering only disappointment and bitterness, both literal and emotional. Crackers that had gone from "salted" to "softened." A forgotten can of condensed milk which, I feared, had begun the process of self-actualization.

There was nothing usable. Nothing inspiring.

The kitchen had been scoured. The landscape mapped, its secrets revealed, its disappointments cataloged.

The biscuit remained. Not a revelation. Not a triumph. But... an option.

A reliable, if uninspiring, option.

And somehow... that was enough.

I returned to the center of the kitchen like a soldier returning from a war nobody declared—not victorious, but alive.

The biscuit lingered in my mind, not as inspiration, but as inevitability. I had fought it, argued with it, questioned it, ignored it. And still, it remained—not loud, not persuasive, just... present.

It wasn't the best idea. But it was an idea.

And in a landscape of indecision and exhausted potential, sometimes that's all that's required. One idea. However modest. However dry.

I stood in the silence of the kitchen, surrounded by the ghosts of better meals and flashier snacks, and I let out a breath—the kind that carries no emotion, only momentum.

Then I moved.

To the pantry. The flour emerged, pale and dependable.

To the cupboard. The baking powder—loyal in function, if not in flavor.

To the fridge—not for answers this time, but for the butter, because even fate needs grease.

There was no ceremony, no swell of music, no grand announcement. Only action. Only inevitability.

And perhaps... fate. Not a dramatic, world-shaking fate, but a small, flour-dusted thread in the great cosmic weave—one that tugged at me gently from the moment the hunger first stirred.

The idea of the biscuit, I now realized, had been seeded long before I ever rose from the couch. It had been waiting patiently, nestled between the folds of possibility and resignation.

Perhaps some part of me knew this would be the outcome all along.

Perhaps the biscuit was always going to happen.

Perhaps that was the point.

I set the ingredients down. Dusted off the recipe card. Took a moment to regard the quiet weight of my decision.

Then spoke aloud, not for drama, but for closure:

"A biscuit it shall be."

CHAPTER 13
Whisking the Void

There comes a moment—quiet, reverent—when the decision has been made, the doubt has been swallowed (though not digested), and the only thing left to do... is begin.

And so I did. I rose from my internal sabbatical and crossed the threshold into the kitchen like a pilgrim reaching the edge of the sacred grounds. Not with excitement. Not with joy. But with the solemn commitment of someone who knows that a journey, however foolish, must at least be seen through.

I began to gather the elements.

Flour. The bedrock. White, silent, and fine like powdered patience. It puffed slightly as I scooped it, like it resented being disturbed. The bag had been opened once before—I couldn't recall when—but it had that familiar folded-top insecurity that said, "You'll probably regret trusting me." I trusted it anyway. I measured loosely, leveling off with the back of a knife that felt too clean for what was about to happen.

Baking powder. The alchemist's spark. The lifter of the low. The one ingredient whose presence is felt only when it is missing. I spooned it in with all the caution of a demolition expert, aware that its powers were disproportionate to its volume. It clumped a little. That felt poetic.

Salt. A pinch, or maybe a judgment. Salt never comes with forgiveness. It is an opinion, ground into crystal. I scattered it with the solemnity of a man salting a snowy road he never intends to drive again.

Butter. Cold, hard, uncompromising butter. Sliced into pieces that looked like currency from an empire that no longer existed. It lay there on the cutting board like forgotten promises—necessary, but indifferent to the task ahead. I stared at it for a moment, debating whether to soften it, then decided that if the butter could survive me, I could survive it.

And finally, milk. Still in the fridge. Still unpoured. I left it there for now, like a secret to be whispered only at the right moment.

I stepped back and observed the counter. Five ingredients, assembled like reluctant prophets awaiting a revelation. A sacred arrangement of edible elements, each containing multitudes.

It struck me, as I stood there—how each piece mirrored some part of myself.

The flour, dry and passive, waiting to be stirred.

The baking powder, volatile and hidden, uncertain if it would rise to the occasion.

The salt, subtle but strong, sometimes too much.

The butter, cold by necessity.

The milk, undecided.

Some recipes begin with confidence, I thought. Mine begins with compromise.

I wasn't sure if I was about to make biscuits or compose a poem I wouldn't admit to writing. But I had assembled the parts. Whatever happened next, it would be something. Maybe edible. Maybe not. But something.

There is a ritual to sifting. A slow, deliberate motion —part grace, part gravity—that transforms a mound of powdered chaos into something lighter, finer, more... manageable.

I took up the sifter with all the gravitas of a philosopher lifting a quill. Into it went the flour. Then the baking powder, hesitantly spooned atop the white mound like a reckless hope. And then I turned the handle.

The clinking, grinding spiral of the mesh below began its patient labor. The flour fell through in drifting curtains—snowfall from a sky with no clouds.

I watched it descend.

Was I purifying the flour, or simply projecting my

internal disarray into a bowl?

There is something to be said for breaking things down into smaller parts. To take the clutter of thought—raw, lumpy, contradictory—and pass it through a sieve of contemplation until all that remains is light, airy dust. Something easier to stir.

Each turn of the sifter handle was a meditation.

What am I doing with my life?

Turn.

How long has this flour been here?

Turn.

Does anyone really know what "well-combined" means?

Turn.

A small clump refused to fall. I shook the sifter. The clump held on.

I shook it again, gently at first. Then with escalating frustration. Still it resisted. It was as if the flour had its own unresolved issues, and this little lump was its inner child clinging to past traumas.

"Let go," I whispered, to both it and myself.

It didn't. I pressed it with a spoon. It smeared slightly through the mesh, defiant to the end. I respected it for that.

Even flour has its resistances.

Eventually, I finished sifting. The powder in the bowl looked different now—lighter, unified, no longer burdened by its own density.

I set the sifter aside, and with it, a small portion of my doubt.

Not all of it. But some.

The butter must be cold.

This was not a suggestion. It was law. Engraved in stone tablets passed down by generations of grandmothers whose wisdom was earned in the fires of forgotten kitchens.

Cold butter, cut into flour—that was the key. The difference between a biscuit and a mistake.

I retrieved the stick from the fridge like an archaeologist lifting an artifact from its tomb. The foil wrapping crinkled with reverence. I laid it onto the cutting board and stared at it for a moment too long.

There were choices now.

A pastry cutter—the device of the purist. Purpose-built. But mine was somewhere in the back of a drawer, wedged between a bent whisk and an orphaned chopstick. Forks? Acceptable, if humble. Fingers? A dangerous path—they warm the butter too quickly, yet offer unparalleled tactile control. The most personal of methods.

In the end, I used a fork in one hand and my fingers in the other, betraying both camps in equal measure.

I began to cut the butter in.

There's a rhythm to it. Press. Twist. Fold. Crumble. A balance between conviction and caution. I worked with the hesitance of someone sculpting fog.

Too much pressure and the butter vanishes—lost in the flour, indistinct. Too little, and the chunks remain —loud, defiant, overconfident in their individuality.

"Too aggressive, and the butter disappears," I murmured. "Too passive, and it dominates."

It felt like something I'd read in a self-help book. Or maybe screamed at myself after a failed relationship.

Flakes formed. Crumbles clung together, then fell apart. My hands moved with uncertain certainty—just enough force to shape, not enough to ruin.

Or so I hoped.

And then—as always—I went one motion too far.

A smear. A softness. A warmth that wasn't there before.

I had overworked it.

Instantly, I was launched into a tailspin of regret. What had I done? Was it salvageable? Was it ruined? Would the biscuits rise in flaky triumph, or sit flat and dense like shame on a baking sheet?

"I knew I should have stopped," I muttered.

The butter didn't respond. It never does.

I stared into the bowl. The mixture was still mostly right. Mostly.

But now I could never not know that I had gone too far.

So I did what every anxious novice does: pretended it was fine and kept going.

The recipe was no help.

"Add just enough milk."

Just enough.

Two words that disguise themselves as guidance but reveal nothing.

Not a measurement. Not a range. A riddle.

What is just enough?

Enough for whom?

For what texture, what consistency, what dream?

I stared into the bowl of flour and butter—the clumpy, uneven terrain of my previous decisions—and held the milk aloft like some ancient elixir. It was whole milk, though part of me wondered if the recipe secretly wanted buttermilk and was simply too polite to say.

I tilted the carton with reverent hesitation.

A splash.

The mixture absorbed it without ceremony. I poked it with the spoon. Still dry. Crumbly. Defensive.

Another pour. Smaller this time. Stirred again.

Now it was too wet. Somehow. Immediately. As if the milk had lied about its volume on arrival.

I stared into the bowl, then into the middle distance.

The room suddenly felt too humid. Was that affecting it? Did that matter? Should I have measured the milk by weight instead of volume? Was the spoon interfering with the texture? Had I tilted the bowl too eagerly, disrupted the subtle alignments?

I was no longer making dough. I was navigating an existential crossroads.

There was a brief but intense moment where I considered going back—rewinding the universe to the flour. Pretending none of this happened. Perhaps starting over with toast.

But I didn't have enough emotional stamina for regret and biscuits in the same afternoon.

So I stirred. Gently. Hopefully. Apologetically.

The mixture came together, but not cleanly. It was lumpy and reluctant. Not dry, not wet—something in between. Something awkward. Something... honest.

I stared at it. The dough stared back.

"Well," I said softly, "you are approximately adequate. Philosophically questionable... but physically viable."

I set down the spoon.

It would have to do.

The moment had arrived—the final mixing.

There was no fanfare. No music swelled. No divine light shone down upon the bowl. Only silence and the subtle weight of commitment.

I took up the spoon—now sticky with residual doubt—and began to fold the chaos.

The flour, once independent and aloof, was no longer itself. The butter, once firm and cold, had been reduced to whispers within the mass. The milk... well, the milk was everywhere, apologetically soaking through what it likely should have only softened.

It wasn't immediate.

There is a moment—imperceptible in real time—when the ingredients stop being ingredients and become something else. You don't notice it until after. Until you look down and realize: this is no longer a bowl of parts.

This is dough.

A singular, stubborn entity born of pressure, chaos, and compromise.

An edible metaphor for self-doubt and hydration.

I stared at it with a mixture of awe and mild resentment.

It had come together. I was proud of it, and yet uncertain whether I had meant for it to become what it was. I had simply... kept mixing. A little more. Then a little more. Until there was no going back.

So many of life's decisions feel like that.

You never see the line until you've already crossed it.

And then you're on the other side, holding something that demands to be finished.

I sighed.

With a reverent hand, I dusted the cutting board—a thin veil of flour, like fresh snow hiding the uneven terrain beneath. I extricated the dough from the bowl, which clung to its walls as if unsure it was ready to let go. Gently, I placed it upon the board.

It slouched there.

Ungraceful. Unshaped.

Much like myself.

I pressed into it—not aggressively, but with something between encouragement and resignation. It resisted slightly, then yielded. I folded, pressed, turned. Not kneading, exactly, but rather... coaxing. Reminding. Reassuring.

"You're doing fine," I whispered, not entirely sure if I meant the dough or myself.

And perhaps it didn't matter.

It was finished.

Not beautiful. Not flawless. Certainly not symmetrical.

But it stood—or rather, it slumped—before me. A biscuit in potential. A lump with purpose. A monument to modest ambition.

I stepped back and regarded my work.

The board was dusted with floury evidence of struggle. The bowl, abandoned in the sink, wore its sticky remnants like battle scars. My hands bore the imprint of effort, coated with the fading residue of something I had made—not perfectly, but earnestly.

"I feared the void," I said aloud, because silence was too loud.

"But now... here I stand, with something vaguely

biscuit-shaped in hand."

And I was proud.

Not because it was good.

But because it was.

It existed.

The product of indecision, of spiraling thoughts and half-measured confidence, of philosophical tangents and emotional detours. It had come through it all, shaped by my hands—tentative as they were.

I placed the biscuit dough carefully onto the baking tray, like tucking in a very tired, very lumpy child under a blanket of parchment.

I turned—ready to face the fire.

The final trial. The moment of transformation.

The oven awaited.

Or so I thought.

My hand reached out with practiced grace, ready to grip the handle and feel the gentle blast of preheated air—the warm breath of progress.

But there was no warmth.

No glow.

No hum.

No heat.

I froze. The tray in one hand. My dreams in the other.

A slow horror crept over me, cold and silent.

I opened the oven door.

Nothing.

The darkness stared back—unlit, uncaring. As if mocking me.

The oven was off.

I had forgotten.

All that effort. All that metaphor. All that meaning...

And the fire, the climax, the alchemical transformation?

Nowhere to be found.

I stared into the void—again. But this time, it was 100% my fault.

There was a pause.

A breath.
Then a sigh. Not of despair. Not of defeat.
But of deeply disappointed acceptance.
I turned the dial.
Click.
The flame roared to life, late to the story but unapologetic.
I placed the tray down on the counter, folded my arms, and whispered:
"Let's see what the heat reveals."
And then I waited.

CHAPTER 14

Preheated Expectations

I didn't panic. That was important.

Yes, I had forgotten to preheat the oven. But anyone could have done that. A minor oversight. A hiccup. Nothing more. I was calm. I was composed. I was—at worst—casually inconvenienced.

I cleared my throat with the forced dignity of a person who definitely meant to wait.

There was no shame in it. Waiting is part of the process. I had simply decided that the dough deserved a moment of reflection before its journey through the fire. Yes. A resting phase. Very culinary.

To keep up appearances, I reached for a spoon—one I hadn't used, didn't plan to use, and had no need to clean—and gave it a thorough rinse. I wiped the counter for the third time, careful to get the corner I always miss, even though there was nothing on it. I opened a drawer, looked at its contents as if I'd forgotten what lived there, then closed it without comment.

This, I told myself, is how professionals behave. They wait, gracefully.

I leaned on the counter with what I hoped was the air of someone who had not forgotten anything. Who had planned this very interlude as an intentional pause. The pose was casual. Elbow on granite, eyes unfocused, head tilted at just the right angle to suggest creative patience rather than abject stalling.

Then I glanced at the dough.

It hadn't changed. Of course it hadn't. It lay there, smug and silent, a lump of hydration and missed opportunity.

I stared at it.

It stared back.

In that moment, I knew that it knew.

To prove I was unshaken, I gave it the smallest of nods. A gesture of mutual respect between creator and creation. "You're fine," I whispered. "Everything's fine."

Finally, as if it were nothing at all, I turned toward the oven and checked the display.

135°F.

A beginning. Nothing more.

I returned to my post, leaned against the counter again. I would wait. I could wait.

After all—what's twenty minutes to someone with nothing but time... and a bowl of slightly judgmental dough?

There's something about heat that refuses to be hurried.

You can press buttons, you can twist knobs, you can set the temperature as high or low as you like—but the oven will take its own time. It does not care for your impatience. It does not speed up to match your hunger, nor slow down to match your hesitation. It simply... becomes.

It is not an agent of chaos. No, it is the opposite—a quiet, unwavering force. It has rules. It has a process. It must reach temperature before transformation can begin. That is the law of baking.

And so I stood in silence, staring at the closed oven door as if it might flinch under my gaze. It didn't. Of course it didn't. Heat is blind. It does not feel the pressure of observation. If anything, I suspected it took longer precisely because I was watching.

"Is preheating," I mused aloud, "just another metaphor for readiness in life?"

The thought startled me. Wasn't that the very thing? We are so often placed into the fire before we are prepared—before we've reached the proper internal temperature to endure what's ahead. And then we wonder why we fall apart, why we burn on the outside and remain raw within.

"You can't rush it," I muttered, pacing now, gesturing with my hands as if explaining it to a ghostly audience. "But you can certainly forget to start it."

I stopped mid-step, stunned by the elegance of the metaphor. Yes. Yes, that was it.

I had forgotten to start.

I had forgotten to start a great many things, actually. Resumes. Apologies. That one novel from three years ago. There was an entire drawer in my mind filled with things I meant to do, meant to begin, but never quite preheated for. They remained unbaked—ideas, dreams, obligations—all dough, no flame.

Surely, I thought, surely the oven is ready now.

I strode over with newfound purpose, filled with the weight of revelation, the grand arc of philosophical reflection behind me. Surely, if nothing else, the universe would reward such patience, such insight.

I bent down and read the display.

158°F.

The betrayal was intimate.

Time—traitorous and slow—had stretched itself into molasses.

No. Not even molasses. Molasses moves.

This was something more sinister: a temporal slog, a soup of seconds refusing to cohere into minutes. I had lived an entire internal monologue and somehow only gained twenty-three degrees. I was beginning to suspect the oven wasn't heating at all, but merely pretending to out of politeness.

And still the dough waited. Not with hope. Not with despair. But with the infinite patience of something that knows it can't do anything about it either.

Time... had shifted.

Not dramatically—there was no great rupture in the fabric of space, no strange temporal anomaly. No, it was more insidious than that. More subtle. Like gravity leaning ever so slightly to the left. Something was off.

How long had it been?

I didn't ask aloud. I didn't want to sound impatient —not even to myself. But I felt it: that growing unease, the sense that I had slipped into a liminal space, a waiting room between realities where nothing moved forward except, perhaps, entropy.

I glanced at the clock.

It read what could only be described as a number. That number was disappointing. It insisted only five minutes had passed.

Five?

Five?

Impossible. I had delivered two philosophical insights, reorganized my emotional failings, and made peace with the slow death of all creative ambition. Five minutes was an insult. Five minutes was a lie.

I stared at the clock again.

It stared back.

I began to suspect the clock was conspiring with the oven. Perhaps the two of them were in communication, keeping secrets. The display on the oven was digital, of course—which only deepened the conspiracy. Numbers, neat and indifferent, blinking back at me like smug pixels of indifference.

172°F.

Progress, allegedly.

I turned back to the dough. It hadn't moved. Of course it hadn't. But somehow, it looked different now —not in shape, not in color, but in attitude. It sat there, squat and lumpy, exuding a kind of smugness. There was a new energy to it—not of grandeur or superiority, but of knowing. Of witnessing.

It knew what I had done.

It knew I had forgotten.

And it was enjoying this.

It was the kind of enjoyment that didn't require sound—the slow, cruel satisfaction of something that need not gloat because your own shame does the work for it. Its silence was louder than any insult. It was a silence steeped in flour and judgment.

And still, the oven whispered on. Low and slow. A

lullaby of inadequacy.

I sank into the memory of every moment I had ever waited. For buses that never came. For test results that carried the weight of futures. For text messages that remained unsent. For someone to say what I needed to hear before I said what I couldn't take back.

Waiting was unnatural. Anticipation was violence by stillness. The human soul was not designed for passive anticipation. We crave motion, progress, something. Even if it's just a timer we can scream at.

I stood again. Slowly. Walked to the oven. Held my breath.

173°F.

One degree.

A single, begrudging concession—not offered, but surrendered under protest. The oven was not cooperating; it was enduring me. Its glowing numbers blinked back with the enthusiasm of a bureaucrat stamping forms in hell.

I had just laid bare the crumbling architecture of my entire psychological interior, and the oven's response? One. Degree.

It was mocking me, clearly—not with words, not even with speed, but with the steady hum of absolute indifference. A metronome for futility. And I, the willing conductor.

A single bead of existential sweat formed at my temple and politely refused to fall.

I turned back to the dough.

Naturally, it was exactly as I'd left it. But somehow, in its stillness, it had gained power.

There it sat—misshapen, pale, and imperfect. A creature of flour and failure. It looked less like something I had crafted and more like something that had always been there, waiting. Watching.

It judged me.

I could feel it. There was no malice in its judgment, only certainty. It didn't need to explain itself. It simply was. The dough did not blink. The dough did not flinch.

The dough knew.

"Is it... drying out?" I whispered.

No response. Just that smug, damp silence. A loaf-shaped middle finger to my uncertainty.

"Is it... relaxing too much?" I asked, this time more pointedly, as if the accusation might force it into confession. "Have I let you go too long, only for you to collapse into a lump of wasted energy and overhydration?"

Still nothing. Just the quiet dough. An edible sphinx.

Then the darker thoughts began to creep in.

"Are you disappointed in me?"

It wasn't an accusation. It was a plea.

I reached for a towel and draped it gently over the dough, as if shielding it from the intensity of my introspection. For a moment, I felt noble. Responsible. I had done a good thing. I had cared for something delicate.

And then—doubt.

Was it too warm now? Would it start to melt? Was it getting too cozy? Would it rise prematurely, or worse—not at all? I removed the towel. Touched the dough.

Was it... warmer than before?

Impossible to tell.

The anxiety returned like a wave, dragging with it a thousand tiny worries. Was the shape wrong? Would it bake unevenly? I knelt down to eye level. Perhaps this side needed rounding out more. Maybe a gentle press here. A loving fold there.

I reached out. Adjusted slightly. Pressed a little. Smoothed.

And immediately regretted it.

It had been, for all its imperfections, a stable imperfection. And now? Now it bore the fingerprints of doubt. Of tampering. Of second-guessing. It no longer looked crafted—it looked interfered with.

I stepped back.

Apologized internally.

Glanced toward the oven. Surely by now it was ready to bring justice and finality to this floury farce.

A blistering 188°F.

I laughed. Not a hearty laugh—not even a full one. Just the dry chuckle of someone who has glimpsed the absurdity of their own helplessness and nodded in solemn recognition.

The dough said nothing. It didn't need to.

It had already won.

What if I just... gave up?

Not in the grand, existential sense—though the temptation loomed—but in the quiet, cowardly way. In the way a person stares at a poorly constructed piece of IKEA furniture and wonders if the floor really needs a bookshelf. Or was it supposed to be a cupboard?

I looked at the dough. Then the trash can. Then the toaster.

Toast. Toast was safe. Toast was quick. Toast required no preheating. Toast didn't judge.

And yet... toast was defeat.

Still, the idea had been planted. My mind, now drunk on possibility, began to spiral. What if I had remembered the oven? What if this entire debacle had unfolded cleanly—dough made, oven ready, biscuit baked, story over? I imagined that alternate timeline—a me who had calmly preheated like a seasoned professional, who now sat comfortably with a golden biscuit in hand, smug and fed.

I could see it: that perfect version of myself pulling the tray from the oven, warm air fogging the glasses I wasn't even wearing, the biscuit rising just enough to be impressive but not so much as to seem arrogant. The butter would melt on contact. The crumb? Flawless. A biscuit worthy of folklore.

But that life was not mine.

Mine was the life of a preheatless fool.

I traced it back—that fatal moment. I could see it: standing at the counter, the flour in one hand, the measuring spoon in the other. The oven only inches away. The button there, glowing faintly, calling out to me like a lighthouse to a ship in denial.

But I ignored it. Or worse—I forgot it.

The act of forgetting feels like a betrayal of the self. It's one thing to make a mistake. It's another to feel it slip through you unnoticed, like time through a sieve.

I turned from the counter and stared out the window.

The sky outside didn't care.

I watched a bird land on the fence, then immediately leave, having presumably realized the fence wasn't warm enough either. I felt that. I was also unprepared for perching.

The dough remained behind me, silent.

I turned back to it, unable to resist the pull of its smug presence.

"I should've made toast," I muttered.

It didn't respond. Of course not. It was dough.

But I felt its disapproval. The subtle wave of disappointment that radiated from its glistening surface like heat from an oven I hadn't turned on. Still hadn't turned on enough.

I approached the oven, expecting—needing—progress.

201°F.

I blinked.

No. That couldn't be right. That had to be a lie. A cruel joke from a machine that understood too well the pain of anticipation.

The number stared back, bold and unblinking.

"That's it?" I asked aloud, not even pretending to direct the question at myself.

I turned slowly to face the dough.

Its silence was no longer passive. It was deliberate.

"You're enjoying this, aren't you?" I asked it.

It glistened slightly under the kitchen light.

"Don't pretend you're innocent. You knew this would happen. I see it in your slouch. In your unearned confidence."

I leaned in, whispering like a conspirator in a church.

"Let's not pretend you're above it all. You're just... dough. You're nothing without me."

And still... it said nothing.

But oh, how loud that nothing had become.

I was pacing again.

It wasn't intentional. My body had simply grown tired of being stationary. I'd already leaned on every viable surface in the kitchen. I'd wiped down the counter twice—not because it needed it, but because I did. I had briefly sat on a stool and stared at the dough, then stood again. Then sat. Then stood again.

I looked at the dough.

It looked... different.

Not in a "miraculous transformation" sort of way. Not risen or evolved. Just... different. Less like a possibility, more like a relic. A lump of beige uncertainty that had, in my absence of action, somehow aged into something more disappointing than dough was ever meant to be.

"Are you still dough?" I asked it.

No answer.

"Because you don't look like dough anymore. You look like... like regret. With a crust."

Still nothing.

I stepped closer, hesitated, then lightly poked the side of the dough with one cautious finger.

It gave a little. Soft. Pliable. Maybe a bit... resentful.

"I'm sorry," I said, genuinely. "That was uncalled for. The things I said earlier."

The dough did not forgive me. But it also did not retaliate, which felt like a small win.

"I'm just tired," I added. "Of waiting. Of not knowing what happens next."

I turned to the oven, needing a sign—some proof that the universe still tilted forward.

305°F.

I blinked. Then laughed—a strange, hopeful sound,

like someone remembering music for the first time in years.

"Oh! We're moving now, aren't we?" I said, smiling. "Look at you, you beautiful radiant box of heat."

I spun—actually spun—with joy. The dough, of course, remained unmoved.

"You see?" I said, gesturing wildly toward the oven. "It's happening. It's finally happening."

I looked back at the dough with a touch of sheepishness.

"And... sorry. Again. For earlier."

I leaned down and gently adjusted a lopsided edge. Smoothed a slight crack with the back of my finger.

"You're going to be fine," I said. "Not perfect, maybe not even good. But you're mine. And I made you. And that counts for something."

The dough didn't answer. But it looked less accusatory now.

Silence returned to the kitchen—not uncomfortable, just... present.

I leaned back on the counter, eyes drifting closed, not sleeping but no longer restless.

"Maybe this is the lesson," I whispered. "You don't always get to do. Sometimes, you just... wait."

And then—ding.

A single, delicate chime. Not shrill, not boastful. Just one soft bell, announcing that destiny had arrived.

I opened my eyes.

350°F. At last.

"...finally," I whispered.

The dough sat ready. Imperfect, but inevitable.

I picked up the tray slowly, reverently—like a pilgrim reaching the last stone step of a winding ascent. My hands trembled, not from doubt, but from the strange gravity of the moment. Of seeing something through.

I turned to the oven.

And stepped forward.

I opened the oven.

The heat rolled out like the breath of some ancient slumbering god, awakened only to judge.

I slid the tray in—slow, cautious, reverent. Like placing an offering. Like laying to rest the body of a dream that might rise again, golden and flaky, or not at all.

The tray settled into place with a hollow metal clink.

I closed the door.

I set the timer.

And I stepped back.

The kitchen had done all it could. I had done all I could. And now...

Now, it was up to the heat.

I looked around—not at the dough (no longer dough), not at the oven, but at the exit. The threshold that led back into the living room. Back to the couch. Back to the phone I had abandoned earlier in the throes of flour and doubt.

I walked to it—slowly, as if parting from an old friend.

I sat down.

Picked up the phone.

Not because I longed for the blue light glow or the infinite scroll of curated banality. Not because I sought knowledge, insight, or even amusement.

But because I could no longer bear to count the fractions of a fraction of a second.

Because staring at the oven would not make the biscuit bake faster.

And silence—true, motionless silence—had grown far too loud.

So I opened a browser. I read a headline. I doomscrolled. I giggled. I groaned. I learned nothing.

But I endured.

And the biscuit—whatever it was becoming—endured too.

CHAPTER 15
The Birth of the Biscuit

The sound was not loud. It was not dramatic, nor melodic, nor even particularly musical. It was a soft ding —a single note, plucked from the instrument of inevitability.

And yet, it echoed like a divine whisper.

I rose before I fully understood that I had risen. My body moved without consulting my mind, propelled by something far older than thought—a primal recognition of completion. The timer had spoken. The biscuit was born.

I moved quickly, but not gracefully. My hand knocked over a spoon, which clattered against the counter and rattled onto the floor. I didn't pick it up. The spoon no longer mattered. Only the biscuit mattered.

The floor creaked beneath my hurried footsteps, each step a verse in a poem that had taken far too long to write. My heart pounded like I was opening a letter with life-altering news. My fingers trembled slightly as they reached for the oven door.

I opened it.

And the heat greeted me like breath from another world—not hostile, but proud. It rolled out slowly, deliberately, as though announcing something sacred. The scent that followed was unmistakable. Not sweet, not spicy, not bold. Just warm. Honest. Earned.

And there it was.

Golden.

Imperfect.

Undeniably biscuit.

It didn't gleam. It didn't glow. It didn't sing with butter or sparkle with sugar. It sat humbly in the center of the baking tray—a lumpy, uneven monument to effort and entropy. And yet... I couldn't look away.

This was it.

The baking was done. The becoming was complete.

The biscuit had arrived.

The oven mitts were already in hand before I remembered putting them on—a strange muscle memory, like saluting a flag or bowing before entering a temple. They were worn, slightly stained, and smelled faintly of past meals... but today, they were vestments.

With the solemnity of ancient rites, I reached into the heat.

The tray clinked softly as I lifted it, careful not to jostle the lone biscuit. It sat in the center, cradled by the parchment like a lone artifact in a museum case—untouchable, delicate, revered.

I moved slowly now. Not out of fear, but reverence. This was no longer just flour and milk and butter. Something had happened in the fire. A change. A metamorphosis beyond mere science.

Yes, there were Maillard reactions and protein coagulations and all the usual culinary suspects. But there was also something else. Something harder to name.

It had endured the fire and emerged changed.

So had I, perhaps.

I set the tray down gently on the counter. The metal rang faintly against the surface—a soft note, like the closing of a chapter. And there it lay, the biscuit, no longer dough, no longer potential. Hot. Vulnerable. Waiting.

I did not move to plate it. Not yet. That honor would come soon, but not now. Now, it had to rest. To settle into itself. To cool, not just in temperature, but in spirit.

And I... I stood nearby, mitts still on, staring down like a parent watching a child sleep for the first time.

Was it ready?

Was I?

I took a breath and let the silence settle in.

I did not sit. I stood near the counter, arms crossed, a

silent sentinel watching over the warm shape of my effort.

It lay motionless, but radiating. Not just heat, but meaning. Presence.

The kitchen was still now. The hum of the fridge, the faint ticking of a clock somewhere beyond, even the whispering air through a cracked window—all of it receded into background noise. There was only me. And it.

The biscuit.

It's strange, how something can feel complete and yet still unfinished. As if the act of becoming was only part of the story—the final chapter unwritten, waiting not in the oven, but in the hand, in the bite.

I leaned forward, eyes tracing every imperfection in its browned, uneven shell. Slightly lopsided. A touch too flat, maybe. But real. Earnest.

So far I had traveled—not in miles, but in thoughts, in feelings, in flour.

I closed my eyes.

And suddenly, there it was.

The dream.

The biscuit, golden like the crown of a proud king, shimmering with butter-born brilliance. Its crust was flaky perfection—the kind that sings softly as your teeth sink into it. Steam curling up like incense from a sacred altar. A richness so profound it echoed back through time, correcting every culinary mistake I had ever made.

It would melt on the tongue. Whisper comfort to the soul. It would—

But then, as dreams do, it shifted.

What if... what if it was terrible?

What if I bit into it and found not warmth, but dry, soulless sawdust?

What if I'd overmixed the butter? What if I'd added too much milk, or not enough? What if I forgot the salt entirely? What if, in all my poetic wandering, I had created not a biscuit, but a monument to mediocrity? An edible disappointment—less dinner and more beige regret?

I blinked. My mouth was dry.

It sat there, unchanged, but now somehow more ominous. A question in carbohydrate form.

Had I done enough? Had I done it right? Was effort enough in the end?

I wanted to say yes. I wanted to believe that the journey justified the result—that intention mattered more than perfection. But the doubts had crept in and taken root like weeds in an untended garden.

My hands trembled slightly. I hadn't noticed.

I took a breath. Slow. Full.

Now is not the time for dreams. Nor for dread.

I placed both hands gently on the counter, grounding myself in the here and now.

What comes will come. And I will receive it.

The decision still waited. But now, I was ready to meet it—whatever it was.

The biscuit cooled. And I... circled.

Not with purpose, not exactly. More like a satellite caught in the gravity of its own uncertainty.

A drawer opened.

Butter. Predictable. Safe. The culinary equivalent of small talk. Reliable, yes, but was that what this moment called for?

Another cabinet. Jam. Strawberry, barely half-full. It felt too eager. Too bright, too cheery, as if trying to mask something. Like laughter after a lie. I shut the door gently, as one would a conversation they weren't ready to have.

The pantry. Honey. Golden and slow. Hopeful. Maybe too hopeful. The sweetness of longing, of wanting this biscuit to be more than it was. More than it might be capable of.

I stepped back.

The biscuit sat unbothered, as it always had. Cooling quietly on the tray, not demanding, not suggesting—

simply being.

This was not a biscuit that cried out for adornment.

But did it deserve it nonetheless?

I leaned against the counter. Arms folded. Eyes narrowed.

What is enhancement, really? Is it an act of elevation, or concealment? A reward, or an apology?

Does dressing something improve it... or hide it?

Was the butter an offering, or a shield? Was jam an act of celebration, or sabotage?

I turned the question inward.

Am I tasting the biscuit... or tasting my fear of simplicity?

Because simplicity is vulnerable. It leaves nowhere to hide. A plain biscuit is a mirror—not for the palate, but for the soul. There is no distraction, no flourish. Just flour, and fire, and whatever lingers between.

I stared at it.

It stared back.

No answers came.

I stood before the biscuit like a philosopher before a button labeled DO NOT PRESS—hand hovering, mind racing, heart pounding with the weight of imagined consequences.

The question hung heavy in the air:

To garnish... or not to garnish?

I closed the pantry.

And then... I stood still.

A calm settled over the kitchen.

Not triumphant. Not relieved. Just... calm. A hush after a storm not because the clouds have cleared, but because I've decided to stop chasing the thunder.

The biscuit was no longer a question. It was no longer a journey. It was not a riddle, a metaphor, a symbol, or a stand-in for my own insecurities.

It was a biscuit.

And that was enough.

I reached for it with the same reverence one might

offer a relic, or a small woodland creature known for biting when startled. I slid the spatula beneath it, gentle, patient, prepared to meet it where it was.

It resisted.

Of course it did.

Clinging to the baking tray like a protester to a cause. As if, after all this, it had the audacity to say, "No. I was not meant for plates. I was forged in heat. I remain."

I jostled. I wiggled. I coaxed.

Finally, it released—not gracefully, but with a begrudging sigh of crumbs. A small scar left on the tray as if to say, "Remember me."

I placed it on the plate, centered and bare. A single moon in a vast white sky.

A napkin unfolded beside it, not as ceremony, but as comfort.

The chair creaked softly as I pulled it back—that same chair that had witnessed doubt and dreams and spirals and snacks rejected.

And then, I sat.

Not to judge. Not to dissect or embellish. Not to wonder what could have been or what still might be.

But simply... to receive.

And there, before me, it waited—not as an answer, but as an offering.

CHAPTER 16
Cooling, Judgment, and Acceptance

The biscuit was gone.

Not physically—not yet. It sat there, still intact in form, still bearing the vague shape and uncertain color of its journey. But something in the moment had shifted. It had crossed the threshold from anticipation to memory, from potential to permanence.

Its fate had been sealed the moment I took it from the tray.

Now, here I sat, not in the flurry of baking or the fevered pacing of the preheat purgatory, but in the quiet that follows creation. The air was different here—still, settled, faintly warm with the echo of what had been. There was no grand epiphany, no crescendo. Just... the biscuit. And me.

It wasn't a bad biscuit. That much needed saying. It was, in truth, precisely what it was destined to be: a product of imperfect choices and honest effort. No more, no less.

There's a kind of reverence we give to food before it's eaten—a final moment of appraisal, as though the act of consumption will erase the evidence of its existence. And so we stare, and judge, and ponder, as if our thoughts can somehow alter the truth of what has already been baked into being.

"This is the biscuit I made," I thought. "And the biscuit I will eat."

It wasn't golden. It wasn't lofty. It hadn't risen into legend or collapsed into disaster. It had simply... become.

Now came the reckoning.

It was the one rule.

The cardinal law of baking.

And I had failed it before I'd even begun.

The oven, that ancient altar of heat and

transformation, had sat cold while I assembled the offering meant for it. I had asked the dough to rise, to take shape, to become—and yet I had not summoned the fire.

How could I have?

How could I forget the most basic of preparations—the single step that stands at the gate of every recipe like a silent sentinel, demanding obedience?

It wasn't just a mistake. It was a betrayal.

Not just of the recipe, or the biscuit, or the gods of culinary guidance.

No, this was deeper—a betrayal of intent, of ritual, of everything that cooking is meant to be. Baking is not improvisation. Baking is covenant. And I had broken that covenant with the quiet, treacherous negligence of not pressing a single button.

The timer had not begun. The warmth had not stirred.

And yet I had moved forward as if it had—as if momentum were enough.

Perhaps I thought effort alone could compensate. That mixing, stirring, shaping would excuse the absence of preparation.

But heat does not bend to will.

It requires patience. It demands attention. It insists on being invited.

And I... I had not invited it.

I wonder, now, how much of what came after was simply the ripple of this forgotten act.

Was the dough too relaxed, too smug in its pre-oven slouch?

Was the crust too pale because it met the fire too slowly?

Would it have risen differently, browned more bravely, flaked more faithfully—if only I had remembered?

Sometimes I entertain the idea of a time machine.

Not to undo some great personal failing, not to

revisit love or loss—no.

Just to return to that moment and press the button that read "Bake."

To light the flame when it mattered most.

Perhaps it wasn't the dough that let me down.

Perhaps it was I—who failed to light the fire.

Of all the culprits—of all the missteps, mishandlings, and culinary sins—there was one ingredient that remained unscathed.

One part of the process that did not falter, did not deceive, did not fail.

The flour.

It was, from the very beginning, pure. Blameless.

Measured with care, sifted with reverence.

Soft between the fingers, like powdered patience. It asked nothing of me but to be included—and I included it wholly, without doubt or delay.

There was no second-guessing.

No spiral of "just enough."

No questioning of temperature or texture, humidity or heat.

The flour was ready.

It had always been ready.

In a world of chaos and overthought, flour is the quiet backbone of baked ambition.

Never the star, never the finish—but always the start.

It does not need recognition, and yet it deserves it.

Because flour holds everything together, even when everything else falls apart.

And this time—even in the face of neglect, of oversight, of ovens unpreheated and butter too cold—the flour remained dignified.

It did its part.

It held its ground.

It became the biscuit, and never once complained about what it had to become.

So I offer no critique. No revisions. No notes.

The flour was not at fault.

It needed no guidance, and it betrayed no trust.

Of all the things I got wrong... I got the flour right.

The butter.

Cold.

Too cold.

Straight from the fridge and full of spite.

I had convinced myself it was the right choice—that cold butter, sharply cubed and cruel, was what the recipe demanded. What the biscuit needed.

But now, in hindsight's merciless clarity, I wonder if I mistook rigidity for wisdom. Chill for control. Logic for understanding.

I cut it in. Brutally. Mechanically.

Pressed it into the flour like I was punishing it for being unyielding, when I myself was the one unwilling to soften.

It resisted, of course. Butter always resists, at first.

But did it crumble properly?

Did I break it down into the delicate shards required for flakiness? Or did I break it apart in defiance—rough, impatient, unfeeling?

Maybe... maybe it was I who crumbled first.

I think now about softened butter—not melted, no, but softened.

The kind left on the counter to contemplate its purpose.

The kind that yields just a little under the knife.

The kind that has been around long enough to know how to blend without losing itself.

Would that butter have understood me better?

Would it have folded into the flour with more grace, more patience? Would it have stayed—not as itself, but as something greater?

I can't help but wonder if I have treated other things the way I treated the butter.

With distance. With rules. With the kind of coldness I justified as discipline.

How often have I expected others to adapt to my

temperature, instead of meeting them where they were?

The butter broke. Or maybe, it simply never had a chance to become.

I didn't give it time. I didn't give it warmth.

I just expected it to perform.

In the end, the butter was in the biscuit.

And the biscuit was in me.

And somewhere, between the two, something didn't quite come together.

Then there was the milk.

"Add just enough," it said.

And then fled into abstraction, leaving me alone with the fear of too much.

There are few phrases in the English language as cruel as those three words.

They pretend to be helpful. Casual. Almost folksy.

But beneath their laid-back charm lies a void—a deep, philosophical canyon of unquantifiable terror.

Just enough for what? For perfection? For cohesion? For survival?

Just enough according to whom?

My grandmother, who baked by instinct and gut feeling?

Or the author of this recipe, who apparently believed divine intuition was a pantry staple?

I poured a little.

Too dry.

Poured a little more.

Too wet.

Somewhere in between lay a moment of equilibrium—suspiciously brief and immediately questioned.

Had I overshot it? Had I dared to believe in balance and been punished for my arrogance?

The dough formed.

But not confidently.

It lingered in a state of false readiness, like someone dressed for a party they weren't quite sure they were invited to.

I remember staring at it, spoon still in hand, trying to determine its truth.

It neither welcomed me nor refused me.

It just sat there.

Pliable but skeptical.

Yielding, but with conditions.

And so began the doubt spiral:

Was it too wet because I stirred too much?

Was it too dry because I hesitated?

Was it all a test, not of my technique, but of my character?

Because maybe—just maybe—the milk was never meant to be measured.

Maybe it was never about teaspoons or tablespoons, or viscosity or absorbency.

Maybe it was about trust.

Madness disguised as methodology.

A final gauntlet thrown down by a recipe that knew exactly what it was doing.

I added what I believed was just enough.

And in the end, perhaps it was.

But I will never truly know.

And that... that is the real cruelty of milk.

But let us not forget the rise and fall of dough pride.

It sat too long. That's the only explanation.

Not long enough to dry out, but long enough to develop a sense of itself.

A dough that once obeyed now harbored... ideas.

Ambitions.

Resentments.

It rose in spirit, if not in body.

A puff of confidence bloomed somewhere within it—unearned, perhaps, but potent all the same.

I hadn't intended to give it so much time.

The preheating debacle, the distractions, the inner monologue turned outer spiral—it all added up to minutes I'll never recover.

Did the dough change while I wasn't watching?

Was this its way of retaliating?

A silent act of rebellion against the one who birthed it, forgot it, and then had the audacity to bake it anyway?

I remembered looking at it, resting on the tray, its edges beginning to settle like it had made peace with its own mediocrity.

But that peace, I now realize, was a mask—the calm before the spiritual uprising.

This was the moment the biscuit decided it no longer needed me.

Not as creator.

Not as guide.

Not even as witness.

Perhaps the biscuit rose too far in confidence... and fell flat in reality.

A cautionary tale in gluten.

And pride.

This was, I believe, the first instance of what I have come to recognize as its quiet defiance.

Not of structure—the biscuit was structurally sound, if uninspiring —

but of flavor, of splendor, of any attempt to be remarkable.

It had decided, without my consent, to be enough... and only barely enough.

Was it punishing me?

For my forgetfulness?

For my sins against softened butter and a preheated oven?

It is not often we accuse baked goods of vengeance.

But I am telling you—that biscuit was no innocent biscuit.

It was birthed with a mission, one forged in the heat of my distraction and shaped in the stillness of my delay.

And its mission was clear: to teach me humility.

A dough betrayed will not forget.

It will rise with pride.

And fall... with purpose.

When I lifted it, it fought.

Not aggressively—no. The biscuit was above tantrums.

But it resisted, firmly, as though affixed not just by heat and flour but by some spiritual adhesive.

As if to say: "Leave me. I was not meant for this world."

It was the final indignity.

After everything—the pondering, the patience, the philosophical unraveling of dough and destiny —

this biscuit had the gall to cling.

Was it overbaked?

Had the tray been too dry, too exposed, too unprepared to cradle its underside?

Or was this simply how biscuits are—born into resistance, baked into stubbornness?

I stared at it for a moment longer, unsure whether to laugh or apologize.

It did not move.

Of course it didn't.

And I began to wonder... was this its final lesson?

That the journey isn't done just because the timer dings, or the heat subsides, or the moment feels complete?

Maybe nothing ever lets go cleanly—not biscuits, not thoughts, not regrets.

Perhaps it wasn't defiance.

Perhaps it was fear.

Of change.

Of relocation.

Of the cold, porcelain unknown that is the plate.

Or maybe—just maybe—it was a flawed crumb structure.

A stubborn bit of browning where the butter and flour had fused into something tougher than intended.

Not deep, not meaningful.

Just... annoying.

Still, I respected its resistance.

After all, I too had clung to my doubts.

To the process.

To the notion that this biscuit had to mean something.

With the flat edge of a spatula and a weary sigh, I pried it loose.

It gave way slowly, with a soft scraping sound—not a scream, not a tear.

Just a quiet surrender.

And then... it was free.

No longer bonded to the tray.

No longer bound to the past.

Just a biscuit.

And I, no longer its maker,

but its witness.

"Next time," I thought,

"I'll preheat the oven before I even consider the flour."

That alone might change the outcome—to greet the dough not with delay, but with fire, before it has time to question its own purpose.

"I'll set the butter out early, let it soften until it knows peace."

No more slicing through chilled slabs like a sculptor desperate for art in stone. Let it breathe. Let it ponder its role at room temperature, where it might blend, not battle.

"I'll demand a measurement from the milk."

No more trusting poetic ambiguity. 'Just enough' is a betrayal disguised as advice—a cruel riddle whispered by recipe writers who want to watch the world burn from a safe distance. I'll use spoons and reason. I'll measure madness into teaspoons.

"I'll knead with purpose, not zealotry."

I'll press with intent, not vengeance. I won't punish the dough for my own insecurities. I'll fold, gently, with a confidence born not from knowing the outcome, but from respecting the process.

And above all—I will not let the dough sit long enough to scheme.

I will cast it into the fire before it has the chance to develop some smug resilience to culinary excellence. No more waiting. No more delay. I will not let it rise into arrogance.

And yet...

Despite it all—despite the cold butter, the vague recipe, the betrayal of the oven, and the biscuit's stubborn refusal to release itself from the tray—this was the biscuit I had made.

Not a marvel.

Not a tragedy.

Just a truth.

Shaped in dough.

Kissed by fire.

And served in quiet reckoning.

I placed it on the plate.

No fanfare.

No final judgment.

Just the quiet understanding that this moment had come.

And with it, the biscuit.

I sat.

I reached out.

And I took it in my hand.

Part Three

A Second Biscuit

CHAPTER 17

The Dough Rises Again

The plate sat where I left it—not ceremoniously, not reverently, just... there. The faintest ring of crumbs clung to its surface like the final notes of a song no one had requested. The biscuit was gone, of course. Devoured. Processed. Digested, at least in theory. And yet, I did not feel finished.

My stomach offered a murmur of approval—the kind of quiet acknowledgment one gives a polite but underwhelming guest. It was not empty, no. But it was far from full. And deeper still, beneath the mechanics of digestion and the faint film of flour still dusted on my thumb, there lingered a more complex hunger.

Not for calories. Not even for flavor.

But for meaning.

I sat there, motionless, listening to the low hum of the refrigerator and the occasional creak of the house settling around me. Time stretched thin in the aftermath, as if unsure what to do with itself now that the Great Biscuit Moment had passed.

Was it simply not enough?

Or—and this thought arrived with the precision of a surgeon's scalpel—was I not enough for it?

I glanced at the empty plate again. It didn't answer. It merely bore witness. Not to triumph, not to tragedy, but to something far more mundane—completion without satisfaction. An act finished, but not fulfilled.

The hunger remained.

And it was no longer clear what it was hungering for.

The hunger had not yet moved to action, but it had summoned a tribunal.

In the grand chambers of my mind—a courtroom furnished with logic, shame, and faint whiffs of baked regret—the trial commenced. I was judge, jury, and unfortunately, defendant. The prosecution stood tall, robed in restraint and self-discipline, fingers powdered with the flour of past indulgences.

"This," they began, "is not growth. This is not self-betterment. This is gluttony dressed in the frilly apron of self-improvement. You are not seeking truth. You are chasing a second helping."

Their words stung with uncomfortable accuracy.

The defense, less confident, but determined, rose with a spatula in one hand and the raw dough of optimism in the other. "Your honor," they said—addressing me, always me—"this is not about indulgence. This is about redemption. The first biscuit was a lesson. The second is a test—not of taste, but of courage. To try again is to hope. To improve."

The prosecution scoffed. "Hope? Or hubris?"

I sank deeper into my seat—a chair in my kitchen, a metaphor in my mind.

"If I make another," I thought, "will it be for nourishment? Or revenge?"

Would I rise at the call of hunger, or merely to spit in the eye of my own failure?

"Is it hunger that drives me," I whispered internally, "or the insult of mediocrity?"

The courtroom fell silent. Even the fridge held its breath.

"What if the biscuit wasn't bland because it was doomed," I mused aloud, "but because I didn't believe in it?"

And there it was—the uncomfortable possibility that the failure was not in the ingredients, nor in the recipe, nor in the laws of thermal conduction... but in me. That my half-heartedness had been inherited by the dough like some genetic disappointment. That a biscuit, like a child, requires love as much as heat.

I rose from the chair, not because the trial had ended, but because I realized something horrifying:

I was considering a second biscuit.

And I didn't yet know... if I was innocent.

I looked at the empty plate again, and for a moment, I didn't see a failed pastry.

I saw a child.

Not a literal one—that would be troubling—but a doughy, lumpy, vulnerable thing that had come into being under my care. A being I had shaped, however poorly, and cast into the fire with all the tenderness of a distracted, emotionally unavailable parent.

I had fed it cold butter and ambiguity and expected it to be warm and kind.

It had no chance.

I pictured it now: the dough, shivering under the weight of my indifference, trying to hold itself together with gluten and hope. Its ingredients were not flawed—they were simply confused. What was it to become, when even I did not know? When my hands were too rough and my heart too absent?

Dough is sensitive. It knows when it's wanted.

You can't rush it. You can't scold it. You can't cut it with a dull knife and expect it not to flinch. You must coax it into becoming. You must show it, in every fold and pat, that it is loved—or at least respected.

A biscuit cannot rise where it is not cherished.

This was not a bad biscuit. It was a misunderstood biscuit. One who came from a home where measurements were vague and the oven unprepared. A biscuit that tried, and perhaps that's all a biscuit can do—all any of us can do—with what we're given.

I hadn't failed the biscuit.

I had failed to raise it.

And maybe, just maybe... I was ready to try again.

The kitchen had gone quiet.

Not empty—not quite. But still. A kind of hush that followed not from peace, but from the held breath of potential. The sound of something waiting to be decided.

The flour had not moved. It sat where I had left it, as flours tend to do—passive, patient, without judgment.

Its silence was not cold, but expectant. Like a book left open on a table, unread but not forgotten.

The oven, too, had cooled. But not completely. I could still feel the memory of fire lingering in its shell—like the echo of a song that had just finished, its last note vibrating in the bones of the room.

The tools were still scattered across the counter, not yet washed or returned to their proper resting places. The measuring cup, with its faint trace of milk; the knife, still bearing the ghost of a butter cube. Nothing had been put away. Nothing had truly ended.

And somewhere inside me, the will stirred again.

Not a roar. Not a vow. Just a flicker—a whisper of defiance against defeat. A soft spark in the ashes.

I looked down at the plate, still flecked with the crumbs of the biscuit that had been.

And I said, aloud this time, "Perhaps... it is time to try again."

Not to erase what came before.

But to rise beyond it.

But first...

There was a mess to confront. A reckoning to be made.

The fragments of the first biscuit lingered—not just on the plate, but scattered like quiet shame across the table, the fabric of my shirt, the folds of my trousers. Tiny echoes of the past clung to every surface, as if to say: We are not gone. We were made. And we remain.

The floor bore its share of shame as well, flecked with flaky evidence of imperfection. It would need sweeping. Perhaps even scrubbing—a cleansing of the culinary conscience.

And the couch?

No. The couch was lost.

Its cushions had swallowed crumbs in silence, sealing them away in the dark crevices where remotes and coins go to commune. To pursue them now would be to wage war on a front already surrendered. The couch had chosen its allegiance—and it had chosen the biscuit.

So be it.

But the rest—the plate, the table, the floor, the clothes, the counter—they could be reclaimed. They could be redeemed. The sins of the first attempt could be wiped clean.

Only then, in a sanctified space, could a new dough rise.

CHAPTER 18
The Cleanup

The biscuit was gone.

Its remnants—a scattering of crumbs, a faint greasering on porcelain, the lingering sense of disappointment—were all that remained. And yet, the kitchen felt altered. Not dramatically. Not in any visible way. But there was a change in the stillness, like the hush that follows an argument no one won. The kind of silence that doesn't wait to be broken, but settles in as something permanent.

I sat still, not out of laziness, but reverence. The act of consumption, flawed though it had been, demanded reflection. I had eaten the biscuit. I had accepted it—blandness and all—into the deepest part of myself. And now the kitchen and I existed in shared aftermath. Neither of us was innocent anymore.

Before me, the plate sat mostly empty. Not clean, no—not yet. But finished. Its purpose, at least for that first biscuit, had been fulfilled. And with that fulfillment came a sort of grief. The knowledge that the biscuit, imperfect and underloved, would never rise again. That whatever hope it had held—of flakiness, of warmth, of buttery transcendence—had been extinguished somewhere between the first bite and the final swallow.

I looked around. The table bore witness to the moment, scarred with scattered flour dust and grease shadows. My shirt wore a few crumbs like quiet badges of failure. The floor had collected its tax—invisible now, but certain to emerge later, mocking me when least expected.

Cleaning was inevitable. But it could not be rushed. This would not be a swipe-and-done affair. No, the crumbs of mediocrity deserved more than that. However disappointing the biscuit had been, it was mine. I had brought it into this world, half-assed and full-hearted, and now I owed it a farewell that was not joyous but just.

To prepare for greatness, one must first remove the ghosts of mediocrity.

Not bury them. Not forget them. But carry them gently to the compost heap of memory, where they might decompose into wisdom.

This was not cleaning. This was ritual.

And so I rose—slowly, as one might rise from a pew after the final hymn—and prepared to sweep the altar of my culinary sins.

I surveyed the scene with the solemn detachment of a general walking the field after a fruitless campaign. The plate was the epicenter, still harboring a few tiny flecks of crust too stubborn to be wiped away by mere gravity. But the real carnage had spread outward in concentric circles of quiet shame.

My shirt bore the first evidence—small, innocent-seeming crumbs caught in the folds between buttons and seams. I brushed them with care, as one might brush dust from a fragile heirloom. They tumbled silently to the table, joining their brethren in the diaspora of defeat.

My lap, of course, had not fared much better. Trousers stained by the powdered ghosts of flour and fat bore silent testimony to poor posture and overly ambitious bites. There was no denying it now: I had become a biscuit mourner, robed in the garments of my own failure.

The table, once a stage for hope, was now a field of quiet ruin. Crumbs of all sizes littered the surface—some large enough to recall the body they once belonged to, others so small they might have been mistaken for dust if not for their unmistakable guilt. Each one a fragment of what could have been. Each one a reminder.

And then, the floor.

The final resting place of the truly lost.

There, beneath the table's shadow, lay the crumbs that had escaped entirely—those who had leaped in desperation, or had simply rolled away unnoticed in the chaos of consumption. They did not beg to be found. They had made peace with their fate.

Some would be discovered weeks from now. Perhaps longer. In the yawning moment between dropping a spoon and retrieving it, in the desperate hunt for a lost earring, or when moving a chair for reasons no longer remembered. But that was their journey now, not mine.

No cleaning was never perfect. Not truly. One can sweep and wipe and scrub, but entropy always wins in the corners. And perhaps that was alright.

Some remnants are meant to linger. A reminder. A whisper. A seed for the next hunger.

And so I acknowledged them—the ones I could see, and the ones I knew I never would—and moved on with what I could clean, what I could control. The rest... I left to the floor and to fate.

The time had come to act. Not rashly, not with haste, but with the solemnity such a moment demanded. The choice of instruments lay before me: a folded napkin, weary and speckled from prior service; a damp cloth, waiting like a priest with absolution in hand; and, of course, the humble hand itself—bare, flawed, human.

Each tool carried its own philosophy.

The napkin was precise, a scalpel in the surgery of spillage. The cloth, more forgiving, more thorough, yet perhaps too eager—wiping history away with a single sweep, like a tyrant rewriting the past. And the hand? The hand was intimate. Direct. A gesture of responsibility unmediated by textile or fiber.

I chose them all in turn.

There is a strange reverence in brushing away crumbs —a paradoxical act of both erasure and remembrance. With every flick of the napkin, I dismantled the remains of the biscuit, but not without recognition. Not without pause. These fragments were not stains to be loathed, but stories to be concluded.

A stain on the tablecloth is a sin remembered. A crumb on the floor, a lesson ignored.

Wiping them away was not cleansing, but consecration. A quiet ritual of redemption. It was not about sterilizing the space—no, that was never the goal. It was about reclaiming it. Making peace with the presence that had lingered too long, and making room for what might come next.

The biscuit had failed to be remarkable, yes. But its memory would not be buried under disinfectant and denial. It would be brushed aside with solemn care, its trail cleared not out of disgust, but devotion.

Even the simplest of tools, in the right hands and in the right mood, can become sacred. And in that moment, cloth and napkin, hand and heart, were unified in purpose.

The altar had been set. The rite was nearly complete.

The battlefield had quieted, the sweeping nearly done. Only a few remained.

Crumbs, scattered like forgotten thoughts, clung to the edges of placemats and the seams between wood grains—survivors of a minor, personal cataclysm. Each one a relic of what was once a whole. And now... it was time to choose.

I spotted it first—the largest among them, roundish, defiant, as though trying to recall the shape of its former self. It rested near the lip of the plate, a reluctant straggler too stubborn to leave. I lifted it between forefinger and thumb, not for nourishment, nor out of pity, but for something subtler—the need to complete a ritual. The final act in a strange liturgy.

I placed it on my tongue.

It tasted of nothing remarkable—flour, perhaps, a vague echo of warmth, the memory of butter like a name almost remembered. But it wasn't flavor I sought.

This was closure.

A Eucharist made of flour and failure.

The others—smaller, indistinct, unshaped—I did not eat. I brushed them gently, one by one, into the fold of the napkin now consecrated by service. Not cast away in shame, but released. Set free from expectation. Their part in the story was done, and not all endings require ceremony.

And then, in a quiet moment by the far leg of the table, I saw it.

The rolling crumb.

Older now. Hardened. No longer fresh in form or meaning, it had become a mystery—a relic displaced by time and gravity. I crouched beside it, considering whether it had waited here all along for rediscovery... or simply fallen victim to narrative convenience.

I left it there.

Not all things need to be reclaimed. Some crumbs were never meant to be biscuits.

The plate was bare.

Not clean—not yet—but bare in the way a stage feels after the final bow, the echo of applause still humming in the curtains. In its center, a faint outline where the biscuit had once rested—a subtle arc of oil, a soft dusting of flour that clung as though unwilling to let go.

It was a ghost-mark. Not of grandeur, but of presence.

I traced it with my eyes, not my hand. Some things should remain untouched in their vanishing. The shape of the biscuit was still there, more clearly now than when it sat in its mediocrity. Its absence had made it... visible.

The plate was empty, yes.

But emptiness is not nothing.

It is the hollow where intention lived.

The negative space left behind by effort.

It is what remains when something mattered—even if it failed to impress, or astonish, or rise.

I stared at the plate not in mourning, but in acknowledgment. This was not loss. This was space reclaimed.

Emptiness is not an end. It is but an invitation to new beginnings.

The kitchen was still.

But not the same stillness it had worn before the first

biscuit—no, that stillness had been rooted in hesitation, in cluttered intentions and unresolved hope. This was different. This was the stillness of aftermath. Of quiet reclamation.

The plate had been cleared. The table wiped. The floor swept with the kind of care usually reserved for guests who never arrive. Crumbs had been exorcised. Surfaces had been sanctified. And though the couch still clung to its small, ancient sins, the rest of the kitchen stood absolved.

The oven sat in silence, as if listening.

The counter no longer bore the residue of failure, but a gleam—not of shine, but of possibility.

The space did not hum, but it anticipated.

Here, now, in the wake of mediocrity, a kind of readiness had formed—subtle, sincere, and profound in its quiet way.

A temple must be emptied before it can be filled again.

And now—now it was ready.

The air was quiet.

The oven now cooled.

The kitchen was ready for the coming of the second biscuit.

CHAPTER 19
A Second Attempt

The bowl was empty.

Not barren—not bleak.

But empty in the way a stage is before a performance, or a page before a poem. A clean emptiness. An emptiness that awaited something.

I stood before it, not as a conqueror, nor a fool, but as someone who had known biscuit and biscuit-related disappointment and returned, wiser and lightly floured.

This was not an act of vengeance. Not a redemption arc.

This was... a gesture.

A promise, perhaps—not to fix what had come before, but to try again with care.

I had been here once before, bowl in hand, heart in throat, butter in fridge. But something was different now. Not just the ingredients—though they, too, had learned a thing or two—but in me.

There was no frantic energy in my motions this time. No romanticizing of outcome. No delusions of grandeur.

Just the soft hum of presence. The quiet trust of practice. The gentle resolve that whispered, maybe, just maybe... this time.

I reached for the oven dial and turned it with a solemn grace, as one might light a ceremonial flame.

"Let it be known," I murmured, "that this time, the fire shall precede the offering."

The sacred preheat had begun.

I returned to the bowl and placed both hands on the counter—not as a chef, but as a penitent. The form of the ritual was the same as before, but the meaning had evolved. I did not wish to dominate the dough into greatness. I wished to invite it.

Flour would come soon. Then butter, softened not by neglect but by intention. Then milk—measured not in defiance, but in faith.

But for now—for just a moment longer—I let the bowl remain empty.

Because before a biscuit can rise, something else must kneel.

First comes the flour.

It had not moved.

Not shifted.

Not stirred in its paper tomb.

And yet, something was different.

The flour had waited—not because it must, but because it could. Time did not insult it. Abandon did not offend it. Flour was not fickle like milk, or moody like butter. It was the monk of ingredients. Cloistered. Constant. Powdered and profound.

I opened the bag and it looked back at me, unchanged. I was not so fortunate.

Before, I had approached it with expectation. I had wielded it. Measured it. Flung it with something bordering on glee, as though to cover the counter in a dusting of purpose. But I had not seen it.

Now, I paused.

I did not measure immediately. I regarded.

Here was an ingredient that had waited for me not to use it, but to understand it. The flour was not merely the start of a recipe. It was the beginning of intent. The unmolded clay of culinary sculpture. The fine powder of promise.

It did not ask questions. It did not offer answers. It simply was.

Flour is not loud in its brilliance. It does not sparkle like sugar or shine like oil. But it is there—in every crust, every crumb, every comfort. The unsung sustainer. The backbone of buns. The bearer of bread's burden. The flake in every croissant's dream.

I sifted it gently, not to soften it, but to honor it.

It fell in clouds.

Not chaotic, but deliberate. Like ancient snow remembering how to land.

And as I watched the flour settle into the bowl, I realized:

It was ready before.

I just wasn't ready to see it.

In its silence, the flour had taught me something.

Some ingredients do not rise. They do not fizz, melt, or bloom. They wait.

And in their waiting, they speak.

Of patience.

Of structure.

Of buns that will be bolder, and biscuits that might dare to be better.

I set the bag aside with reverence, not because the flour had changed—but because I had.

And so the foundation was laid.

Soft. Steady. Unshaken.

Flour—the quiet architect of the rise to come.

Now we come to the butter, no longer cold and contemptuous but soft and graceful with an elegant beauty of yellowy forgiveness.

The butter had not resisted.

There was no clatter of knife against cold slab. No struggle to cleave it from its chilled exile. No brittle defiance. It had been waiting—not idly, but becoming.

Softened.

Not weak, but willing. Not melted into chaos, but supple in its surrender.

I touched it, and it yielded without protest. It did not shatter. It did not sulk. It belonged.

There was a time—not long ago—when I would have praised its coldness. Called it integrity. Structure. Strength. But now, I saw the truth: the butter had not changed its nature. Only its readiness.

I had left it out that morning, not by accident, but by choice. I had placed it with care. Let it sit. Let it breathe.

Perhaps that's all some things need—not force, not urgency, but space to warm.

It didn't resist this time.

Perhaps neither did I.

I cut it with gentleness, folded it in with reverence.

No longer was it a battle of textures, a war of crumbs and force.

Now it was a communion—a melding of softened resolve and floured foundation.

It did not dissolve. It became.

And as I watched it fold into the dough—its golden hue vanishing into the pale heart of flour—I set aside a small piece. Just a sliver. Just enough.

I would melt it later, blend it with a pinch of the sacred—basil, garlic, maybe thyme if it felt right. Not to flavor over, but to honor through.

A final touch.

Not a decoration. Not a topping.

A crown. For a biscuit that would not be praised for flair, but for flavor.

The milk remained a riddle.

It sat there, blank-eyed and opaque, offering no wisdom, no measurements, no signs. It did not shimmer with knowing, nor swirl with intention. It simply... was.

But I had changed.

There was no tremble in the hand, no furrowed brow as I poured.

"Enough," I said. And this time, I believed it.

This wasn't the milk's redemption. It was mine.

I did not wait for a sign. I did not plead for clarity.

I measured—with spoons this time, but also with faith.

Not the blind faith of desperation, but the hard-earned faith born of mistakes made, crumbs mourned, and a biscuit chewed in silent reconciliation.

Was it enough?

Yes. Not because it was measured, but because I was present.

And perhaps—just perhaps—that is the true madness of milk:

It cannot be defined. Only accepted.

Poured not from precision, but from peace.

I stirred it in with a calm heart and a wary gut—the latter offering a quiet reminder that wisdom, like lactose, sometimes comes with consequences.

Still, this was no longer a moment of fear.

It was communion.

This wasn't about avoiding too much.

It was about embracing just enough.

A splash more—not too much.

A pause—not too long.

A smile—soft and real, like milk in motion.

And when it was done, I looked into the bowl, not for reassurance, but out of gratitude.

The dough was becoming. The path was forming.

And the milk—the milk had meant something.

Before the hands came, there was the salt.

Small, crystalline, bitter as memory—it slipped into the bowl with the quiet conviction of one who has always been misunderstood. It did not seek glory, nor sweetness. That was never its role.

Salt, after all, is the great balancer.

Too much, and it dominates. Too little, and everything else forgets itself.

It is the unsung friend who tells you the truth even when it stings—because it must.

And in that sting, there is trust.

Some people are like salt, I thought.

Sharp-tongued. Bracing. But necessary.

They don't ruin the dough—they reveal its depth.

And then came the baking powder.

Soft. Pale. Easily mistaken for flour until it is not.

It did not shout. It did not sparkle.

But with it came the promise of ascent.

This was the alchemy of grace.

A pinch of soda to lift what could not rise on effort

alone.

It didn't force the dough upward—it reminded it that it could float.

We stir it in and forget it, but it remembers its task.

It is the quiet faith that, in the right heat, all things might rise.

Only then—only once all was gathered—did I place my hands into the bowl.

Not like before.

There was no frenzy. No vengeance.

No desire to subdue.

Just touch.

Just presence.

The dough welcomed me. Or perhaps it always had, and I simply hadn't noticed.

I pressed and folded, not to change it, but to coax it.

To meet it halfway.

There are things in life that yield when battered —

But dough?

Dough yields when invited.

With each press, I breathed.

With each fold, I listened.

It wasn't about domination.

It was about understanding the difference between shaping something and breaking it.

"Not every task requires force," I whispered.

"Some simply require presence."

And so I stayed.

The dough, warm and pliant beneath my fingers, rose in spirit—not yet in body—as if recognizing that this time, it was not being taken.

It was being known.

The oven was ready.

Not as an afterthought. Not as a last-minute redemption.

It had been preheated with purpose.

This was forethought made flame.

I stood before it, holding the dough with both hands

—not as a sculptor admiring his work, but as a parent offering up a child to the world, knowing the world had been made ready to receive it.

To cast the dough into fire is cruel,

unless the fire has been made to receive it.

And this fire?

It welcomed.

There was no sullen hiss of cold metal waking too late.

No impatient waiting for the glow to reach its fullness.

This was readiness incarnate.

The oven door opened not with screech or reluctance, but with a breath—like the exhale of a monk who has waited years for this moment of enlightenment.

I placed the biscuit upon the tray. No hesitation.

Not dropped. Not flung.

Placed.

Centered, reverent.

As if this tray were no longer just steel,

but altar.

There was no ceremony.

And yet, it was the most ceremonial thing I had ever done.

The door closed.

And the fire took it—not hungrily, but faithfully.

Not as punishment, but as promise.

The heat enveloped it with the careful balance of passion and discipline, as if it, too, had learned something since the last time.

This was not vengeance.

This was intention.

And so, I waited —

not with pacing, nor peering through the glass like a panicked baker chasing perfection.

I waited with quiet. With breath. With trust.

For I had done all I could.

The biscuit's fate no longer lay in my hands.

But in the hands of the flame —
a flame that, this time, I had lit with love.
I did not pace.
There was no tapping of fingers, no squinting at timers, no twitch of impatience.
I watched. That was enough.
Through the oven's glass—fogged faintly with the breath of effort—I saw it begin to swell.
Not in haste. Not with bravado.
But with quiet confidence.
It rose.
The dough, once so formless, once so doubt-ridden, now lifted itself—slowly, humbly—as if unsure whether it was allowed to become.
But it did.
It rose.
And I, too, rose—not from my seat, but from my doubt.
A part of me, once sunken in the regret of a first attempt, now found lightness.
The oven light glowed soft amber.
It was not just heat.
It was hope.
A warmth not just for the biscuit, but for the one who dared again to make it.
I pressed a hand gently to the oven door. Not to rush it. Not to interfere.
But simply to be near—to share in the heat, to offer presence, not pressure.
"If it rises, it rises," I whispered. "If not... it still becomes."
The scent filled the air: butter, flour, a whisper of salt.
It curled around the kitchen like a memory being made in real time—gentle, present, purposeful.
I thought of the mistakes.
The cold butter. The uncertain milk. The zealot's kneading. The late oven.
Each now not a wound, but a scar—healed,

instructive.

This was no longer about redeeming the past.

This was about honoring it.

A tear formed, soft and unspoken. Not out of sorrow.

Not even joy, exactly.

But something like peace—the kind that comes when you know you've tried again, not to prove worth, but to accept it.

The biscuit swelled slightly more. A golden tint kissed its surface.

It was not perfect. I did not need it to be.

But it was becoming.

And I...

I had become, too.

The timer did not ring.

It chimed.

Not a harsh alarm, but a soft reminder—that something was ready.

I approached the oven with the kind of quiet typically reserved for churches and birth rooms.

There was no fanfare. No internal drumroll.

Just breath... and butter waiting to fulfill its final role.

I had prepared it beforehand—not in haste, not in desperation, but with intent.

A small saucepan had melted the softened butter into golden silk.

To it I added the gentlest touch of garlic—not to dominate, but to speak in whispers.

Basil, too—a green breeze of herbal memory.

And thyme... a pinch, perhaps for its name alone, for it reminded me that all things come with it, and so few things wait without it.

And so I took the biscuit from the oven.

It did not gleam. It did not beam with holy light.

It was simply... what it was.

And this time, that was enough.

The top, lightly golden—a soft brown blush of self-awareness.

Its form humble, its height modest, its scent divine.
It did not ask for praise.
It asked only for presence.
And so I gave it that.
With brush in hand—not a ceremonial scepter, but it felt like one —
I anointed its crown with the prepared butter.
Not doused, not drowned, but kissed —
lightly, reverently, with the yellow blessing of understanding.
The herbs clung like emeralds.
The garlic shimmered faintly in the warm embrace.
It was, at last, not merely a biscuit, but the biscuit —
a creation not of desperation, but of quiet grace.
I placed it on the plate—clean now, ready, sacred in its simplicity.
No grand speech.
No imagined parade of kings or critics.
Just breath.
And a pause.
"It is what it is," I whispered. "And this time... that is enough."
The kitchen did not cheer. The world did not shift.
But something in me, once fractured by flour and flawed intention, felt whole.
There would be a bite, yes. A first bite.
But not out of hunger. Not out of proof-seeking.
Out of peace.
And perhaps... a bit of love.

CHAPTER 20
A Better Biscuit

It did not arrive with fanfare. There was no sudden scent that overtook the senses, no golden spotlight through the window to illuminate its crust like a halo. No, this biscuit came quietly. It simply was—placed before me without ceremony, without apology.

And yet, I felt it. Not the heat—not yet—but the promise of it. A kind of radiance that lingered just beneath the surface, like a candle behind a curtain. There was no need to touch it to know it was warm. The air around it had shifted, softened—as if the room itself had made room for it.

This biscuit does not shout.

It whispers.

And I am ready to listen.

The plate beneath it, once a stage for disappointment, now bore it like a throne bears a monarch. Not a conqueror, but a ruler of quiet integrity. No lavish garnishes, no showy dollops of cream. Just the biscuit. Alone. Unadorned. Whole.

It sat slightly off-center, as if by accident. But I knew better. Nothing about this felt accidental. It had been crafted—not for perfection, but with intention. And that intention, now fulfilled, radiated outward like heat from a hearth.

I inhaled—not sharply, not ceremonially. Just enough. A breath not to brace, but to receive. There was no need for defense. No expectation to temper. The war of the first biscuit was long past. What remained now was the peace earned in its wake.

I did not marvel aloud. I did not cry.

I simply looked.

And in that still moment, I understood:

A perfect thing need not announce itself.

Its stillness speaks louder than pride.

It radiated warmth—not the kind that warns, but the kind that welcomes. Like sunlight filtered through a clean windowpane, late in the afternoon, when the world has nothing left to prove. My fingers hovered above the surface, then rested there, gently, as if not to press but to learn.

The crust crackled faintly beneath the pad of my thumb—a dry whisper, brittle but not sharp. Not fragile. Just finished.

Edges once feared for their burn were now kissed with caramelization. Crisp ridges, where butter had met pan and made something more of itself. They weren't even. Of course not. But that's what made them beautiful. Each ridge and rise, each golden shelf of crispness—they formed a terrain, not a template. A range of tiny mountains, browned with triumph, not overdone but overcome.

The gloss... oh, the gloss. It wasn't a shine like syrup or varnish. It was more like a sheen of purpose. A light brushing—not drizzled, not drowned—of the butter that had been set aside, melted with reverence, and stirred with subtle intention. Garlic, softened to near invisibility, left only its scent behind, while flecks of basil held their shape like runes inked into pastry.

I traced one with my eyes, not my finger—some sacred texts are not meant to be touched.

And beneath it all, the dough. Pale gold, flaking in soft shelves, rising in gentle layers like pages not yet turned. It bore no scars of haste, no wrinkles of regret. The folds were quiet. The rises were proud. This biscuit had not been forced to be beautiful. It had simply been allowed to become so.

I turned it slowly in my hand—not to judge, but to witness.

And in its curves and edges, its ridges and glints, I saw not flaw, but formation. Not accident, but attention. Not perfection by symmetry, but by soul.

Perfection isn't the absence of irregularity—it's the

presence of care.

And this biscuit had been cared for.

I lifted it with both hands—not out of necessity, but reverence. This was not a thing to be plucked casually or cradled without thought. It had heft, and that heft mattered.

It settled into my palm with quiet authority—not heavy, not light, but right. Like a stone pulled from a riverbed after years of current and erosion, shaped not by design but by the patient insistence of time. Its rounded edges bore no sharpness. Its weight gave no resistance. It rested there willingly, as if it, too, had waited for this moment.

The bottom was golden. I turned it gently in my hand and let my thumb press against it. Firm, but not hard. Resilient. Like a memory that no longer stings, but still holds shape.

And at the top—the crumbly crown. My fingers brushed across it with the lightest trace, not to test, not to prod, but to remember. I had made this. With thought, with care, with softened butter and chosen patience. Every flake was a monument to the moment I had let go of control and simply... tended.

It crumbled slightly beneath my touch, and I did not mourn the loss. Some things are meant to break. The joy is in the holding, not the having.

This time, the weight doesn't hint at disappointment.

It hints at fullness.

The biscuit bore its own history, and I bore mine. And in that meeting—warm dough against warm hand—there was no tension. Only gratitude. I did not clutch it. I held it. As one holds something earned. As one holds something that holds them back.

The things we carry should not crush us, but ground us.

And this biscuit, this golden, humble thing—it grounded me.

I did not rush. Not this time.

The biscuit, now warm in my hand, rested just shy of my lips. I let it pause there, suspended—not to tease myself, but to honor what had come before. A small smile found its way across my face. It did not stretch wide, nor quiver with giddy anticipation. It was soft. Real. The kind of smile that lives close to the heart.

Memories stirred—not sharp-edged regrets, but softened echoes. I remembered the first biscuit. Not with embarrassment or bitterness, but with a quiet bow of the head, as one might offer to a portrait of an ancestor. It was that first failure, after all, that shaped the hands now holding this biscuit.

This moment did not ask for hunger. It asked for presence.

I stood still. The room was still. And yet, everything vibrated—faintly, invisibly—as if the walls themselves were holding their breath. There was no ticking clock, no humming fridge, no distant passing car. Just warmth. Just waiting. Just the sense that something was about to become.

I do not wait because I fear the truth.

I wait because I respect the moment.

Time did not slow. I did.

This was not the fear of disappointment. This was the reverence of recognition. I had been here before—but not like this. I had rushed, once. Bitten too soon. Judged too quickly. And I had learned.

Now, the stillness spoke. It did not ask for words.

When we learn to trust the silence, we finally hear the song.

And the song was playing now—quietly—beneath the surface of the biscuit, the surface of the moment, the surface of myself.

Still I waited. And in that wait, I was fulfilled.

The biscuit rose—slowly, deliberately—as though it were not lifted by my hand, but drawn upward by gravity reversed. By intention refined.

It did not resist. It arrived.

As it neared, the air changed. Heat radiated off its

surface in gentle waves, like the breath of something living—not hot, but warm, close, welcoming. A halo of thyme drifted upward, carried on a breeze no one had summoned. Butter followed—soft, sweet, earthy—a perfume steeped in patience and fire. There was a whisper of garlic, but not too much. Just enough to remind me that joy, too, can be grounded.

I paused, but not in hesitation. There was no fear here. Only reverence.

A breath rose in me, then caught—not from surprise or tension, but instinct. My lungs, it seemed, understood what my mind had not yet said: This is sacred.

In some moments, our body understands what the mind has not yet spoken.

My fingers adjusted subtly, not out of clumsiness, but affection—like adjusting a frame around something precious. My eyes closed, not to conjure fantasy, but to feel more completely.

Darkness sharpened everything else.

The warmth at the edge of my lips.

The scent, now fuller, rounder, alive.

The heartbeat in my fingertips.

The silence, still holding, still humming.

Nothing was rushed. Nothing was wasted.

The biscuit hovered, not in suspension, but in invitation—an offering given not by fate or fortune, but by effort. A ritual nearing its climax.

And still, I waited... for just one beat more.

There was no fanfare.

Just a sound—the softest crack, crisp and clear, like the opening note of a symphony tuned only for one. Not brittle. Not dry. A breaking, yes—but not a shattering. A yielding.

The crust gave way as though it knew it must. Not under pressure, not from force, but from invitation answered. It did not resist; it parted. Not like glass, but like petals. Like a blossom at dusk.

Some things fall apart. Others fall open.

A flake—featherlight—drifted free, caught briefly on my lip before falling to its final rest on the plate. Another settled on my tongue ahead of the rest, a herald of what was to come. And then—the rest of the bite, whole and warm, followed through.

A hum escaped me.

I had not meant to make a sound. I had not thought I would. But something within, long quiet, stirred. It wasn't pleasure in the loud, boastful sense—not glee, not celebration. It was recognition. A greeting from the soul to the senses:

There you are.

No more questions. No resistance. No stern judgment of moisture or crumb. The bite was simply right. Not because it met every expectation, but because it asked for none—and still delivered more than I had hoped.

I smiled. "It did not fight back," I thought. "It invited me in."

My teeth met not defiance but welcome. The texture was soft beneath the crackle, like silk under armor. And there, just there—a whisper of thyme. Not shouting. Just reminding me that effort, when laced with care, leaves a trace.

One moment. One sound.

And I knew this was not the same kind of bite.

This was fulfillment.

Before taste, there was touch.

The biscuit rested on my tongue like it belonged there—not as a guest, but as a returning traveler. Warm. Present. Humble.

It did not crumble into defiance or dust. It held itself together, just enough, before yielding—flake by flake, layer by layer—each part parting like the pages of a story I had once read but never truly understood. And now... now I did. Not because the words had changed, but because I had.

The crumb was moist, but not wet.

Tender, but not fragile.

There was structure here—not rigidity. It held its shape only to offer itself more fully. It met the pressure of my palate like a hand held just long enough to be known, and then released with trust.

I pressed the bite gently against the roof of my mouth. It gave way. Easily. Earnestly. Without resistance. And for a moment, I did nothing more than feel.

Even my tongue seemed gentler now, as if it too had learned not to judge too soon.

This was not the chalky burden of a biscuit left too long or loved too little. This was forgiveness in physical form. This was care, remembered through texture.

I did not rush to taste. There was time.

There was grace.

The texture of grace is not smooth—it is kind.

And kindness, here, could be felt.

It began, as many joys do, with something familiar.

Butter.

Not loud. Not boastful.

It simply arrived—rich, warm, and whole. Like a memory made real.

It did not melt into the biscuit—it had become it. The two were inseparable now. The butter had not been added, but absorbed—folded into the very being of the bite.

Then came the garlic.

Not the loud garlic that declares itself in every dish—but a quiet breath of it, trailing beneath the butter like a secret. A murmur in a cathedral. Present, but not pressing.

And basil—oh, the basil.

It did not cut through. It danced beside. A brightness, a lift. Complexity without conflict. A reminder that even comfort can contain curiosity.

And finally—salt.

A single note. Placed with purpose.

Not shaken, but chosen.

It was the period at the end of a sentence—no more, no less.

The final note of a sonata that needed no encore.

The bite did not crash like cymbals. It expanded. Like warmth in the chest. Like a smile that begins in the soul before it ever touches the face.

I thought flavor would strike me.

But it didn't.

It embraced me.

There were no tears—not because it wasn't worthy, but because it asked for none.

There was almost laughter—not at the biscuit, but at myself. For doubting this moment would ever come.

Instead, I breathed.

Full. Slow. Present.

True joy does not erupt.

It expands.

And this biscuit—this beautiful, impossible, golden miracle—was joy.

The bite was swallowed.

No fireworks. No choirs.

Just warmth.

Settling.

There was no need to dissect. No urge to rank.

No scale against which this biscuit must be measured.

It did not need to be the best.

It only needed to be real.

And real it was—in every buttery layer, every flake still clinging to the edges of my mouth. A biscuit not defined by grandeur, but by grace.

This biscuit was good.

Not just better.

Good.

The plate beneath it, once a sterile arena of culinary trial, had become something gentler—not a battlefield of judgment, but a cradle of effort. Of intention. Of care.

I looked at it, not with greed, not with critique, but with gratitude.

A whisper escaped—soft enough that only the biscuit could have heard:

"Thank you."

Not to the flour. Not to the butter.

Not even to the biscuit itself.

But to the effort. To the second attempt.

To the version of me that had tried again.

For a long time, I simply sat there. Breathing. Whole.

And then, like a gentle wind rustling through the curtains of contentment, came a question:

Was this biscuit truly better...

or was I?

Had it risen higher, flaked finer, tasted deeper...

or had I merely learned to notice, to savor, to accept?

Was the first biscuit truly bland—or had I been unready to taste it?

Perhaps this biscuit is not better in every way.

Perhaps only slightly.

Perhaps not at all.

But I am.

And perhaps that is the true miracle —

that growth can be flavored into flour,

that redemption can be folded into dough,

and that peace can be baked into a biscuit.

Still, one bite is not enough to know.

So I lift it again.

And prepare for another bite.

Not to doubt.

Not to question.

But to know truth.

The truth of the flour—bold, determined.

The truth of the butter—within and upon.

The truth of the milk—too little, too much... or just enough.

The truth...

of the biscuit.

CHAPTER 21
The Second Second Bite

The biscuit had changed.

No longer pristine, no longer untouched—a corner was gone, carved away by intention. What remained was asymmetrical, slightly softened at the edge where teeth had once met crust. It was not ruined. It was not diminished. It was, simply, different.

And that difference... felt right.

There is a strange dignity to a thing once it has been used—not abused, not broken, but engaged with. The biscuit now bore the mark of memory. It no longer waited to prove itself. It had already begun the story.

A familiar shape altered. A golden roundness now interrupted. But in that absence, I saw not loss... but history.

The first bite had been an awakening—a revelation. But this moment was quieter. Calmer. I did not marvel. I did not gasp. I looked, and I understood.

The symmetry was gone, yes—but what is symmetry, if not the illusion of perfection? The missing piece did not unbalance the biscuit. It gave it character. It gave it context. It told me, without words, something has happened here. And it mattered.

I studied the empty space like an archaeologist might study a missing shard from a once-whole vessel. But unlike the shattered relics of ancient civilizations, this biscuit was not broken. It was becoming.

I traced the edge with my eyes, noting the exposed layers within—soft, golden, inviting. It no longer asked to be judged. It invited me to remember.

No two bites are the same. I had said that once, early on. But I had not yet known why.

Now I did.

Because no two moments are the same. No two selves

are the same. And no bite—no matter how perfect—can ever truly be repeated. It can only be continued.

A small breath settled in my chest. Not heavy, not expectant—just... full.

I looked at the biscuit again, altered and at ease, and thought:

What's missing from a thing can say as much as what remains.

Not wounded. Not flawed.

Just... changed.

And in that change, something sacred remained.

The interior had been revealed.

Where once there had been only crust—golden, glossy, and proud—there was now a new landscape: soft, porous, and full of quiet detail. I leaned in without hesitation this time. There was no doubt, no fear of blandness or collapse. Only curiosity. A calm, deliberate curiosity.

The crumb rose and fell like gentle terrain, not uniform, but purposeful. Each pocket of air spoke of effort—not flaw. I studied the structure as though I were peering into a cross-section of earth itself, a layered record of time, temperature, and trust. This was not the shell the biscuit presented to the world, but the soul it kept safe beneath.

Tiny golden flecks glittered just under the surface—remnants of butter that had seeped in and caramelized inward, as if the richness had traveled deeper to hide where only the brave would look. And I had looked.

It reminded me, strangely, of ancient bread—the kind discovered in tombs and ruins, fossilized by time, studied not for consumption but reverence. A preserved testament to craft and sustenance. Except this biscuit was not a relic. It was alive, still warm from the oven, still tender from the making. And its story had just begun to unfold.

I ran a finger lightly across the edge of the bitten side. The crumb yielded softly beneath my touch. Not fragile, but forgiving.

Was this the true biscuit?

Not the crust, not the sheen, not the basil jewels or the garlic perfume—but this?

This warm, spongy, structured interior?

Maybe.

Maybe the biscuit had always been more honest on the inside.

Maybe it was never trying to dazzle. Only to endure.

Sometimes, what's hidden holds more truth than what's shown.

And truth, once hidden, has a way of emerging when it's ready—not when we demand it.

In the first biscuit, this moment had sparked hesitation—the fear that what lay beneath would not live up to the promise of what was seen. But this time, there was no such fear.

Only trust.

Not blind. Not naive.

But earned.

The bite had opened more than just a crust.

It had opened a dialogue.

And I was finally listening.

When I lifted the biscuit again, it was—of course—lighter.

Not by much. Just enough to notice. Just enough to feel the change not in the hand, but in the expectation of the hand. A subtle imbalance. A slight lean. The center of gravity had migrated, pulled away from where it once belonged. It did not fight me. It simply shifted.

My fingers, without thought, adjusted their grip. A thumb slid closer to the edge, the index curled in more tightly beneath the remaining bulk. A micro-drama, barely visible, yet precise—the kind of instinctive adaptation we make a hundred times a day but only notice in stillness.

And this was stillness.

I paused.

The biscuit was no longer whole—and that meant it

was no longer neutral. It had a history now. A tilt, a curve, a story. The shape I held was no longer sculpted for symmetry or presentation. It was sculpted by experience. By contact.

And it still fit.

Maybe even better.

It sat in my hand not like something diminished, but something defined. No longer a vague promise of potential. No longer a blank canvas. It was a known thing now. Changed, yes—but not broken.

Some things aren't broken. They've simply shifted.

There was a quiet gratitude in that thought—for the unevenness, the adjustment, the intimacy of knowing how to hold something that isn't what it used to be.

In the past, I might have lamented the imperfection. The missing corner. The lack of clean lines. I might have turned it, studied it, mourned what was gone.

But now?

Now I felt the weight not as loss, but as clarity. I knew this biscuit. I knew what it had given me. And I held it accordingly.

And so, even as it grew lighter—even as it leaned —

it never once felt like it might fall.

There was no trembling this time.

No breath held hostage, no prayer whispered into the steam. No silent negotiation with the gods of grain and dairy.

I remembered.

I remembered the first bite—the one that cracked gently, sang softly, and settled into my chest like the warmth of sunlight through a window. That bite had surprised me. This one... awaited me.

And yet I did not feel less for it.

Is joy made less joyful by memory? Or more sacred?

I sat with the biscuit in my hand, still warm, still inviting—but not unfamiliar. Like returning to a favorite bench beneath a tree you once wept under. It's different now. Not because the tree has changed, or the bench. But because you have.

I smiled, not in anticipation, but in appreciation.

A brief thought wandered in—uninvited, but not unwelcome.

Are second kisses sweeter?

Sometimes. When the first one was clumsy and full of fear.

Are second episodes better?

Only if the pilot didn't try too hard.

And the second sunrise after heartbreak?

That one... yes. That one often is.

I chuckled—not aloud, just a vibration in the breath. The kind of laugh that's shared only with oneself and the occasional biscuit.

In the early pages of this tale—if we dare call it that—anticipation had been a pedestal. A hallowed pause. The breath before the music. And rightly so. But continuation... continuation has its own dignity.

To remain.

To return.

To still want the thing after you've known it once.

There's love in that. Perhaps more love than in wanting it the first time.

Perhaps joy does not come from novelty... but from the return.

The biscuit did not shimmer with mystery anymore. But it radiated something deeper.

Welcome.

I lift the biscuit once more.

It is lighter now, uneven. The edge where my first bite claimed its truth is no longer clean—not torn, but altered. Not ruined, but reshaped. A small overhang of crust juts like a crag, catching the kitchen light in a way it never did before. It glints not with glory, but with honesty.

A single crumb clings to that edge—a fragile stowaway resisting gravity and time.

For a moment, it holds. Then, quietly, it lets go.

I watch it fall with a sort of ceremonial sorrow. Not loss—no, not that. Just the quiet farewell of something that once held on and now does not. A soft end. A gentle descent. A speck of memory made motion.

The biscuit no longer looks dignified. Its roundness, once whole, is now fractured. But somehow, this shape—this jagged crescent, this imperfect arc—feels more worthy than before. More lived-in. More true.

"Symmetry is repetition. But this jagged edge tells a story."

And it does.

The story of a first bite taken with reverence.

Of butter basted not as decoration, but devotion.

Of a hand steady with memory, not with hunger.

The shape has changed.

The ritual has not.

I close my eyes again—not to dream, not to imagine some flavor yet to come—but simply to feel what is already here. The air, warm. The biscuit, near. My hand, sure.

This is not the anticipation of the unknown.

This is the return to something known—and still sacred.

The biscuit reaches my mouth—no fanfare, no drumroll, only breath and intention.

This time, it is the interior that greets me first.

No crust to announce the moment with a crackle or crisp defiance—only the soft, warm yield of the crumb. It gives without resistance. A hush in place of a trumpet.

Then, only afterward, the crust arrives. A frame, not a barrier. A finish, not a guard. The reverse order of the first bite, as if the biscuit now trusts me enough to reveal its heart before its armor.

A fragment breaks loose, unexpectedly—a loose petal of crumb that rolls toward escape.

But I am ready.

My tongue, reflex trained by reverence, catches it with the quiet grace of someone who has been here before. No panic. No surprise. Just recovery. Natural. Honest.

Not a flaw.

A reminder.

Even good things crumble sometimes.

And yet, even in its collapse, there is no regret. The texture is softer than before—not limp, but yielding. Like a door that was once stuck and now swings open without a sound.

This second bite is not about conquest.

It is about welcome.

"It did not fight back. It invited me in—again."

And I accepted it, with an open mind and an open mouth.

The bite does not linger.

No grand finale, no curtain call—just a soft dissolution, as if the biscuit knew its role and played it with graceful brevity. The crumb gives way quickly, almost too quickly, like a word spoken once but understood forever.

It is gone before I can cling to it.

But not before I feel it fully.

A small fragment lodges between two teeth. Not painful. Not disruptive. Merely... present. A stowaway of satisfaction.

I smile.

Not annoyance, but amusement. A gentle hum of humanity in an otherwise poetic moment.

Perfection, I realize, is allowed to be playful.

This bite was not longer than the first.

It did not demand attention or rewrite reality.

But it stayed with me—in the taste, in the texture, and yes, in the tiny imperfection it left behind.

This bite didn't last longer... but it stayed with me.

And somehow, that feels like more.

The flavor arrives not as a revelation—but as a return.

Butter, bold and round, emerges again—not louder, not sharper, but clearer. It does not surprise me this time. It greets me, like an old friend met in a quiet room.

Basil lingers at the edge of the tongue. Garlic dances just behind it. A rhythm remembered, yet richer. I don't marvel at the complexity now—I recognize it.

Recognition is its own kind of wonder.

Then the salt—that perfect, precise punctuation—lands again, not as a flourish, but as structure. It holds the sentence together.

I've tasted this before, and yet...

It's like rereading a passage and finally catching what was always there.

Each flavor, familiar—but this time, understood. Not as parts, but as a whole. Like a chord once heard note by note, now heard in harmony.

There is no doubt now.

No wondering if my hunger colored the experience, if the contrast of blandness made delight seem sweeter.

This was not the echo of novelty.

It was not gratitude painting taste with false gold.

This was not illusion. This was real.

The bite settles.

There is no grand finale. No triumphant crescendo.

Only the soft exhale of something real.

Nothing in me rushes to name it.

I do not analyze the ratio of crust to crumb. I do not measure its success against the shadow of the first.

If the first bite was a question... this was an answer.

Not the final answer. But an answer nonetheless.

And in that—I feel something loosen. Something small. Something human.

The plate before me is no longer the stage of a saga.

No longer a battlefield, nor a confessional.

It is simply a plate. Holding something good.

Goodness does not always need to be earned. Sometimes, it is simply allowed.

And there, in that quiet moment, a whisper settles into me.

Not from the biscuit, but from the journey.
The first bite gave me hope.
The second gave me proof.
And yet...
I find myself wondering...
Was the biscuit better?
Or was I?
Or had we both—somehow, quietly—risen?
I lift the biscuit again.
Not to judge.
Not to doubt.
But to know.
The truth of the butter.
The truth of the milk.
The truth...
...of the biscuit.

CHAPTER 22
Nothing Left to Prove

There was no pause between bites.

No voice in my head questioning the choice, no internal narration explaining the motion. Just the natural continuation of something right. My hand moved. My mouth welcomed. And the biscuit answered, as it had before—with quiet confidence and no hesitation.

This was not indulgence. This was not restraint. This was... flow.

I chewed without rush. I swallowed without ceremony. And before the thought could form, I was already lifting it again.

The second biscuit did not need to prove itself. It had already spoken. I was not eating to analyze, nor to compare. I was not searching for deeper meaning hidden between the flakes.

I simply ate.

And for once, that was all I needed to do.

There was no need to narrate.

No need to prepare for each bite with ceremony or thought.

I was already in it—the rhythm, the cycle, the quiet song of presence.

Bite.

Chew.

Pause.

Breathe.

Again.

No interruptions. No inner monologue weighing flavor against memory. No need to ask what this bite meant, or whether it meant more than the one before. I did not need to think between bites. I only needed to chew.

It was not mindless. No, far from it. It was mindful in the truest sense—not full of thoughts, but full of awareness. My jaw moved not with hunger, but with gratitude. My breath came not in sighs or startles, but in soft, steady currents that kept pace with the biscuit's gentle unraveling.

I did not measure the size of each bite.

I did not consider how much remained.

I did not prepare myself for the final one.

Each moment was its own, complete and sufficient.

Each pause a settling of the spirit.

Each breath a soft agreement: Yes, this. Again.

There are some meals that ask to be remembered.

This one asked only to be experienced.

And so I did.

Bite.

Chew.

Pause.

Breathe.

Again.

There were no scattered fragments, no brittle trails marking where the biscuit had been.

No battlefield of flaky casualties. No apology of shattered crust.

Only a flake or two—delicate, deliberate—resting on the plate like punctuation.

A golden speck near the edge. A soft sheen where butter had once pressed.

It left almost nothing behind.

And yet, it left everything in me.

I recalled, without judgment, the first biscuit's aftermath —

the lonely scatterings, the crumbled confusion, the vague disarray of a promise not quite fulfilled.

But this... this was different.

This was a biscuit that knew how to arrive.

And more importantly—how to leave.

Not with a bang. Not with a mess.//
But with grace.

It didn't try to cling. It didn't need to linger to be remembered.

It left space behind, not to be filled, but to be honored.

And I, too, felt no need to pick at the crumbs.

They had already given what they came to give.

There were no wrong bites.

No lesser ones, no flawed corners.

Not a single mouthful that felt forgotten or rushed or reluctant.

Each bite arrived with the same quiet confidence, the same subtle grace.

The same fullness.

There was no need for commentary now.

No internal ranking, no scoring of layers or textures or flavor distribution.

It was not a biscuit that begged to be praised—only eaten, fully, attentively.

Bite by bite by bite.

I chewed. I breathed. I continued.

Not because I was driven to finish,

but because it deserved to be finished.

No part of the biscuit tried to impress.

And none held back.

Each bite gave what it had.

And each time, that was enough.

It sat between my fingers, small enough to vanish in a single motion, yet heavy with the weight of every bite that had come before. The final morsel—not just of this biscuit, but of the hours, thoughts, and quiet revelations it had given me.

I turned it slowly, watching how the light traced its uneven edge. A crust that promised a crisp welcome. A soft interior that had invited me in without hesitation. A golden seam where butter had chosen to linger. It was no different from the bites before it, and yet... it was all of them at once.

For a moment, I did not think of eating it. I thought of holding it forever, a perfect fragment suspended at the edge of completion. But perfection does not live in preservation. It lives in its fulfillment.

I drew a breath, not to steady myself, but to honor the quiet gravity of the moment. This was not a bite to be rushed, nor delayed.

It was simply... waiting.

The final bite was gone before I could think to name it. No farewell, no fanfare—just the quiet meeting of what was and what is.

The plate before me was bare. A white expanse broken only by a few harmless specks, too small to chase, too perfect to disturb. In that emptiness, there was no loss.

I did not feel full. I felt finished.

There was no part of me that longed to go back, to stretch the moment beyond its shape. The biscuit had given everything it had to give. I had received it. We had ended together, as we should.

The room was still. My hands rested. My breath was unhurried. The plate was clean. So was the moment.

The last fragment waited in my fingers, light and perfect, free of even a single crumb. I placed it into my mouth, letting it rest there a moment before it dissolved into what it had always been—warmth, butter, and quiet joy.

There was no more biscuit. But there was no sadness.

No part of me reached forward in want, and no part of me looked back in regret.

The plate, once a landscape of absence, was now simply clean. Clean in form. Clean in feeling.

The biscuit was gone. And so was my hunger. In every sense.

CHAPTER 23
Final Reflection

The first biscuit began, as all things must, with the first bite. Not a glorious one. Not one to linger in the mind for years or inspire ballads of buttery splendor. But it was honest. The crust, faintly flaky and faintly bland, introduced itself without pretension. It did not lie about what it was, nor did it apologize for what it was not. There is a kind of comfort in that—the comfort of knowing exactly where you stand, even if where you stand is in the middle of mediocrity.

The crumbs came next, and with them, a quiet revelation. They were not the kind of crumbs that topple civilizations or ruin days. They were small, ordinary things—scattered flecks across the table, the lap, the shirt. And yet, they persisted. Days later, one would still emerge from a fold in the fabric or the shadow of a placemat. In their own way, they proved that even the humblest of beginnings can leave a lasting trace.

The journey continued into The Mid-Biscuit Plateau, that inevitable stretch where novelty fades, and the remaining distance to completion looks longer than it is. The plateau is not about flavor, nor hunger—it is about will. And will, I discovered, is often measured not in leaps, but in the refusal to stop walking.

There were distractions, of course. The knock at the door, the errand from nowhere, the package of wool socks hardly worth the pageantry of a delivery signature. The phantom ring from the living room that led to no caller and no message. These were interruptions, but also seasonings—not of spice or salt, but of narrative. Without them, the story of the first biscuit might have been less human.

And then, Too Late for Butter. A revelation born of hindsight, the kind that arrives not when it can change things, but when it can only stand beside them. Regret settled in—not heavy, but present. I had eaten the biscuit without the garnish it perhaps deserved, and in doing so had learned something quietly important: regret does not always spoil what came before. Sometimes, it lingers as an aftertaste—not sweet, not bitter, but unmistakable. I know now that regret tastes different when it is edible.

It began before the first bite, before the oven's glow, before the flour met the bowl. It began with hunger—not the heroic, chest-clutching hunger of a man starved by circumstance, but the quiet, polite kind. The kind that could be ignored, but refuses to leave the room. A hunger that says, "I could wait... but why would I?"

This is where the first fridge check came in. That initial opening was done with the full expectation that the chilled shelves would greet me with inspiration—a revelation in Tupperware, a leftover that felt just right, a sudden stroke of culinary destiny. What I found instead was an unremarkable assortment of dairy, condiments, and a produce drawer in a state of questionable intent. I closed the door, unimpressed, but certain that my answer lay elsewhere.

The second fridge check came minutes later, though I had not added a single new ingredient to my kitchen. This is the realm of magical thinking—the belief that, somehow, in the span of a commercial break or a passing cloud, the fridge will have reorganized itself into a banquet. I opened the door again, and once more, found no such miracle. The same jars and cartons looked back at me, only now they seemed mildly irritated at being inspected twice.

And then, the third fridge check. This is the moment of surrender, where you admit that you may have misjudged the food you already own. A jar of jam that looked uninspiring before now seems like a potential cornerstone. Eggs you dismissed earlier begin to suggest themselves in whispers. It is not that the contents have improved—only that your standards have lowered, or perhaps your perspective has shifted. This is where reason loses, and invention begins.

From there came the pantry—the "graveyard of options" where once-loved ingredients had gone to expire in the shadows. Here lay the half-empty bags of flour, the sugar container that had been full for so long it might qualify as an antique. I gathered them not with excitement, but with resignation, as if conscripting reluctant soldiers for a war neither of us wanted.

And then, Whisking the Void. A strange transformation took place. My idle hunger had become ritual. The motions—sifting, measuring, whisking—began to feel purposeful. I was no longer merely passing time; I was building toward something, though what that something would be was still uncertain. In this, I suspect, lies the danger and the beauty of making anything: once you begin, you cannot help but hope.

The oven preheated—Preheated Expectations. It hummed with the promise of transformation, that quiet alchemy where cold dough becomes warm bread. Yet I couldn't help but think of the many times I had forgotten to preheat entirely—that universal misstep of the impatient or distracted baker. Those times when you slide the dough into an oven still coming to life, and in doing so, rob it of the conditions it deserves. The heat never arrives in the right way, the bake suffers, and so does the spirit.

Preheating, I've learned, is not just about the oven—it's about readiness. About making sure the conditions are set before you begin. It's the unseen work before the visible work, the part that never makes it into the recipe's glamor shots. This time, the oven was hot, the stage prepared. And because it was prepared, my mind was already racing ahead to the taste, the texture, the triumph. I imagined a biscuit so perfect it would erase the memory of every dull meal before it. And because I had imagined so much, the reality could only fall short—but that was a lesson I would not fully grasp until much later.

And yet, The Birth of the Biscuit did not bring defeat. It was not what I had pictured—it was smaller, plainer, quieter. But it was real. In a world where much remains imagined, there is a certain grace in the thing that actually arrives.

Finally came Cooling, Judgment, and Acceptance. The biscuit rested, and so did I. I understood, then, that creation rarely matches expectation. And yet, the act of making—of pulling something from the nothing—remains its own quiet victory. This, I think, is why we return to the kitchen, to the workbench, to the page. Not because we expect perfection, but because sometimes the making itself is enough.

The Dough Rises Again was not just an act of baking—it was an act of return. I had been here before, in this kitchen, at this counter, standing over a bowl of dry ingredients. But this time, there was a difference. I was not simply following the motions to make food; I was making a promise to myself. A promise that I could come back to the same place and leave it better than I had before.

The Cleanup from the first attempt had been more than sweeping crumbs and rinsing bowls. It was the purging of a past that, while not a failure, was far from fulfillment. The countertop no longer bore the ghost of the first biscuit's mediocrity. In that cleared space lay the possibility of something new—not perfect, perhaps, but better.

And then came the Second Attempt, lived again scene by scene, step by careful step. I remembered the little mistakes from before—the oven preheated too late, the flour measured without enough attention, the dough handled with just a touch too much force. This time, I adjusted. I didn't overhaul the process into something unrecognizable. I simply learned from the first round without letting those lessons turn into overcorrections. The salt stayed in balance. The butter was worked in evenly, but not aggressively. The dough was shaped with respect, not manhandled into submission.

There's a strange thing about first attempts: when they fail, you feel the sting. But when they succeed—truly, perfectly succeed—there's an emptiness to it. A hollow cheer that fades faster than you expect. The real satisfaction, I think, comes not from getting it right the first time, but from having to try again. From knowing that you've carried something forward, refined it, and made it yours.

It made me wonder—what's the point of a first attempt if you're never going to use it as a stepping stone to something greater? Why gather lessons only to let them rot in the back of your mind like forgotten vegetables in the crisper drawer? And yet, I have done this more times than I can count.

There was the guitar I bought with the intention of learning just enough to play a single song—still sitting in its case, strings slack from neglect. The half-finished model ship gathering dust on the top shelf, its sails forever unraised. The short stories that start strong, only to trail off into blank pages, abandoned because the early spark fizzled.

But the biscuit—this second biscuit—would not meet that same fate. I had returned, not out of obligation, but because the first attempt had taught me something, and I was finally ready to use what I had learned.

The dough rested. The oven waited. And so did I—patient, deliberate, certain that this was not just another try, but the proof that I could follow through.

It did not arrive with fanfare. There was no chorus of angels, no theatrical gleam in the kitchen light, no smug announcement from the biscuit itself declaring its superiority over all others. The perfection of this biscuit was quiet—so quiet, in fact, that I might have missed it had I been looking for spectacle instead of substance.

The first bite told me everything I needed to know. Not in a shout, but in a whisper that somehow filled the entire room. The crust gave way with just the right resistance, its warmth cradling the unmistakable, generous presence of butter—both within and upon, as though the biscuit had been infused with kindness at every stage of its making. It was the kind of bite that needed no defense, no argument, no persuasive essay.

The Second Second Bite carried with it the briefest flicker of doubt—the kind of doubt born not from imperfection, but from disbelief. Was the first bite simply an overreaction, an exaggerated relief from the mediocrity of the first biscuit? I chewed slowly, listening for any betrayal in the flavor, any flaw in the texture. None came. If anything, the second bite was better than the first—deeper, fuller, more certain. The biscuit was not trying to be good. It simply was.

And as I ate, I realized there was nothing left to prove. Not to myself, not to the biscuit, not to the phantom critics I sometimes imagine watching from the corners of my mind. The perfection here was not fragile, not something that could shatter under the wrong kind of scrutiny. It was sturdy, like truth, and truth does not require applause.

This was the continuation I had been hungering for —not the continuation of eating, but the continuation of being present in the act until its natural conclusion. I had not only avoided the mid-biscuit plateau, I had walked straight through the heart of it without ever losing momentum. There was no stall, no lull, no moment of staring off into the distance and wondering if I should pause or push on. I simply ate. And in eating, I completed what I had begun.

When the last bite was gone, there was no ache for more, no itch for a third attempt, no regret over what might have been. The plate, once a battlefield of crumbs, sat clean and calm before me. It was not empty. It was finished.

And in that stillness, I understood something that all the unfinished projects, abandoned hobbies, and half-written stories of my life had never taught me: completion is not the enemy of ambition. Sometimes, to move forward, you have to allow something to be done—fully, finally, without noise.

It occurred to me, as I sat with the last lingering warmth of the biscuit still echoing faintly in memory, that perhaps this—this very act of remembering—had become as meaningful as the biscuit itself. The story was now not merely about a thing that happened, but about the telling of it. Like replaying a conversation with an old friend, only to find the act of replaying it becomes the new conversation, overwriting the original.

In some quiet, ridiculous way, the reflection had taken on its own life. I began to wonder—when I think back on this day, will I remember the biscuit, or will I remember remembering it? Will I sit here years from now and reflect upon this very reflection, peeling back layer after layer of memory until the biscuit itself has vanished completely, leaving only the shape of the thinking it inspired?

It is entirely possible—and here I must smile at the absurdity—that the biscuit will live longer in the loops of my own mind than it ever did in my hands. And if that is true, then perhaps I have eaten not just a biscuit, but a self-replenishing meal of thought, destined to be revisited, reheated, and served again whenever I wish.

And so the reflection becomes the story, the story becomes the memory, and the memory becomes the biscuit—a perfect, infinite loop in which the act of remembering is itself the nourishment.

Today I ate a biscuit. It was, truthfully, the most remarkable of biscuits. The crust, though modest, was golden and confident. The butter—bold, unmistakable—was both within and upon. Every bite knew what it was and asked for nothing more. And still, it gave. A biscuit that promises little but delivers much is not just honest—it is generous. And there is a kind of peace in generosity, especially when it arrives without pride.

And with that, I set down my fork, pushed in my chair, and left the table. The meal was over. The story, perhaps, would never be.

About the Author

From an early age, Justin M. Davis found joy in shaping stories that blend emotion, imagination, and introspection. Writing became both a creative outlet and a quiet space to explore the complexities of thought and experience. What began in childhood grew into a lifelong pursuit of understanding life through narrative.

Justin's work is marked by philosophical undercurrents and emotional depth, crossing genres as the story demands. He writes humor, mystery, and epic fantasy with equal care, unified by vivid worlds, grounded characters, and a reflective, thoughtful voice.

His debut, Today I Ate a Biscuit, began as a simple experiment—expanding a small, ordinary moment into a narrative of unexpected meaning. He is also the author of the upcoming fantasy series Sophie's Journey and the psychological thriller Ace of Spades, each exploring different facets of human struggle and inner truth.

When not writing, Justin enjoys time with his family, composing music, creating video games, and practicing light nature photography—creative pursuits that often find their way into his work.

www.ingramcontent.com/pod-product-compliance
Lightning Source LLC
LaVergne TN
LVHW040147080526
838202LV00042B/3052